# The Three Rules of Everyday Magic

Amanda Rawson Hill

BOYDS MILLS PRESS
AN IMPRINT OF HIGHLIGHTS
*Honesdale, Pennsylvania*

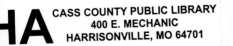

For my Grandma and Grandpa Rawson,
who showed me that though the mind may forget,
the heart plays on

## Acknowledgment

Jane's poem on page 59 is "Where I'm From" copyright © 2017 by Joan He. Used by permission of the author, who controls all rights.

Boyds Mills Press
An Imprint of Highlights
815 Church Street
Honesdale, Pennsylvania 18431
boydsmillspress.com
Printed in the United States of America

ISBN: 978-1-62979-940-7 (hc)
ISBN: 978-1-68437-149-5 (eBook)
Library of Congress Control Number: 2018934188

First edition
10 9 8 7 6 5 4 3 2 1

Design by Tim Gillner.
The text of this book is set in Berling LT Std Roman.
The titles are set in Blooms Regular.

# Part I
## Believe

# Chapter 1

There's something about that moment right before the first star appears in the sky. It's like at an orchestra concert when the conductor raises his hands and everyone is hushed, not even breathing, waiting for that very first note to wash over them.

*At my first concert with Dad, the conductor paused on the stand for what seemed like forever. It went on so long I couldn't help wiggling in my seat.*

*"Patience," whispered Dad. "The music's coming. I promise."*

I lean back against the rough bark of an almond tree, feel the chill of the breeze across my face, and hear something like those words again. Except this time it's my best friend, Sofia, saying them.

"It's coming, Kate." She rubs her thighs to warm them up. "It won't be long now. I promise."

Sofia gets a daily email about the night sky and when

certain stars will appear. It's never wrong. Ever. But that doesn't mean Sofia can't remember it wrong. I'm about to say so when she shouts, "Look! There it is!" She points at a bright star hovering above the orange line of the horizon.

I look at my watch. "Right on time."

Sofia laughs and bumps her shoulder against mine. "Told you. Make a wish."

We both close our eyes, scrunching them as tight as we can. The scrunching part is very important when making a wish. I hold my breath, and those words come back to me again. *The music's coming. I promise.*

But the only person who can bring the tinkling, crashing, zipping, soaring sound of music back into my life is Dad. "Please, please, please," I whisper.

Beside me I hear Sofia mumble, "*Por favor.*" I open my eyes and see her clasping the cross hanging from her neck.

"It's not a prayer, you know."

Sofia opens one eye. "Sshh. You're breaking my concentration."

"What kind of wish are you making?"

"A big one. Obviously. Now quiet." She rubs her thumb along her cross a couple more times, mouthing something I can't make out before sighing and looking at me. "There." She drops her necklace.

"Why were you praying?"

"It never hurts to try everything. Not when it's important."

The wind blows again, finding the spaces between the buttons on my sweater. I can't see buds forming on Mr. Harris's almond trees yet, but they'll be there soon. It's the beginning of January, and spring always shows up the first week of February. You can count on it.

"So what did you wish for?" I ask. "To go back in time and have Christmas again?" It's the last Friday of winter break. There are probably a lot of people wishing for that right now. People who didn't open all their presents with one eye on the door waiting for someone who never came.

"And be cooped up in the house with Marcos and Miguel for another week?" says Sofia. "No, thank you. My wish is much bigger and more exciting." She presses her lips together the way she does whenever she has a surprise treat for me in her lunch box.

"Tell me!" I poke her arm. "You have to tell me."

"I don't know. Then it might not come true."

I roll my eyes. "You don't actually believe that."

"You're right." Sofia laughs. "I'll tell you. I wished to be a movie star. With a mansion and a closet full of beautiful dresses and somebody I pay to clean my room."

I glance at the bottom of Sofia's jeans where her mother sewed in cotton lace to make them long enough for her to keep wearing. "You're right. That's a big wish."

Sofia stands up and begins waltzing around and waving at imaginary people. She speaks with a snooty British accent. "When my movie premieres, you'll accompany me down the red carpet. It will all be very fancy."

I wrinkle my nose at the word *fancy*.

"Don't be like that!" Sofia says, her British accent faltering.

"What? I just don't want to wear a fluffy dress or anything stupid like that."

"It's not stupid." Sofia curls her hands into fists the way she does when she's about to yell at her brothers.

I jump to my feet. "Maybe I can come as your bodyguard."

Sofia's hands unclench. "I guess that would be okay."

"Then I can karate chop anyone who gets too close."

"Yeah! *Hiyah!*" Sofia does her best impression of a roundhouse kick, but she is way off.

I relax into ready position with my fist resting against the palm of my other hand. "Nobody touches my best friend. These hands are registered weapons."

"That's right." Sofia calls into the night, "Watch out! She's a black belt!"

"Well, not yet."

Sofia goes back to waving at imaginary admirers. I shove my hands into my pockets. "You still won't wear pink on the red carpet, right?"

"No way!" Sofia holds out her pinkie to me. "Never wear pink and best friends forever."

I wrap my pinkie around hers, and we shake on it. There's a rustle from somewhere in the orchard behind us, and we both jump. But it's just Mr. Harris's cat. He meows and rubs against my leg.

"Sorry, Fred," I whisper. "No milk for you. Mr. Harris said it's making you fat and lazy." Fred saunters off between the trees.

"Come on," says Sofia. "Let's go inside. It's freezing out here."

We trudge through Mr. Harris's almond orchard, ducking beneath branches so they don't catch in our hair.

"So are you going to tell me what you wished for?" asks Sofia.

At the edge of the last row of trees, the dirt turns to gravel crunching beneath our feet, and we can see my house. "I wished for my dad to come back."

"How long has it been now?"

"Four months and seventeen days."

Sofia doesn't act like it's weird that I know exactly how

long it's been or tell me that it's never going to happen. Because that's not what best friends do. Instead she stops on my front porch, turns around, and loops her arm through mine while we look at the star one last time.

"That's a big wish," she whispers. We stay that way for a few moments, with our wishes swirling around us and floating up into the sky like smoke from a bonfire.

# Chapter 2

*T*hat night, after we're both in our pajamas and Sofia is snuggled into her sleeping bag on the floor, she says, "I'm going to try out for the play at the downtown theater next week. Marisa Nunez is doing it, too. She told me at church."

"Oh yeah. I forgot you guys go to the same church now."

"I want you to do it with us."

"I don't know." My karate trophies sparkle in the light from the hallway. "What about karate?"

"Rehearsals start at six o'clock. You're done with karate by then, aren't you?"

I prop my head up. "What do you have to do for tryouts?"

"Well . . ." Sofia's voice trails off and she pauses. The darkness crowds in closer. "It's a musical. So you have to sing a song."

I flop back onto my pillow. "Nope. No way."

"But you used to love to sing."

I look at my black guitar on its stand in the corner of my room. The darkness hides it, but I know there's dust around its edges. Dad would be mad about that if he knew. I remember the first lesson he gave me.

*"A guitar is an instrument, a tool, and a friend," Dad said.*

*"A friend?" I giggled.*

*"Of course." He leaned in close, his forehead touching mine. "You treat it right and it will treat you right."*

*Mom peeked around the corner of the room. "Mothers are the same way you know."*

*"All beautiful women are like that." Dad stood up, walked over to her, and gave her a long kiss, smiling afterward.*

*"Ew! Gross!" I yelled.*

I wish I could see that again. Not the kissing. Just the smiling.

I shake my head. "No. No singing."

Sofia's sleeping bag crinkles as she moves around and grumbles. "Of course not."

"Are you mad at me?"

"You never do anything I want to do."

There are some lies said so many times your whole body seems to understand. My fingers curl into fists. "That's not true."

Sofia sighs. "Whatever. I'd do karate if . . ."

*If we could afford it.* That's what she was going to say. But Sofia tries to never talk about her family's money problems, even though that's exactly the sort of thing best friends are for.

"I know," I whisper.

I can't stand this feeling. Like there's a giant weed growing up between us. I roll over and stare out my window. The star I wished on earlier is still out there, just barely. It hangs right above the edge of the hills. I know it's not really a star. It's Venus. Mom likes to point it out every time we drive home from karate. But my heart whispers something Sofia said earlier. *It never hurts to try everything. Not when it's important.*

*Please*, I say in my head. Maybe to Venus. Maybe to God. Maybe to the air. I'm not really sure. *Please bring my dad home.*

Venus just winks back at me. Sofia's breathing is soft and long, with the tiniest whistle. That's how I know she's asleep. I reach under my bed and pull out the orange shoebox waiting there for me. The lid slides off, all flimsy and soft from being touched too much. Inside the box is a sparkly purple pen, a bunch of notebook paper, and thirty-seven folded notes.

I started writing the notes after Dad left. Before the depression came and Dad stopped looking at me, he'd sit on the edge of my bed every night. We'd play our guitars and sing. He'd ask about my day. Sometimes, we talked so long Mom would have to order Dad out of the room.

But now he's gone. Sometimes the words and the thoughts and the music I don't sing anymore swirl all around my brain. And when it feels like I can't hold them in anymore, that the words might roundhouse kick a hole straight through me, I write them down on a piece of paper, fold it up, and put it in the shoebox. Because one day Dad will come home.

He'll want to read these letters when he does.

I take the cap off the sparkly purple pen and begin to write.

♪ ♪ ♪

*Dear Dad,*
Wynken, and Blynken, and Nod one night
Sailed off in a wooden shoe.

*I remember singing those words together. Your voice was low. Mine was high. We both sang slow so I could get my fingers set just right for each chord.*

*I tried singing that song to myself after you left but it sounded all wrong, and I haven't sung anything since then.*

*I won't sing without you. I can't sing without you.*

*Love,*

*Kate*

# Chapter 3

"**G**irls, get up. Get up, get up!" Mom's voice calls us from the door as she switches on the light.

I groan and pull the blanket over my face. "Why? It's Saturday."

"There's been an emergency. We need to go. Now."

I bolt upright, fingers pushing into the mattress. My mind thinks a million thoughts about Dad and something bad happening. I want him to come home, but in a happy way. Not a sad way. "What is it?" I ask.

Sofia sits up, too. She brushes her dark brown hair away from eyes as big and wide as the day her dad got heatstroke and had to go to the hospital.

Mom marches into my room with both of our shoes and tosses them on the floor by the bed. She's already dressed in jeans and a sweatshirt, but her hair is frizzy and sticking out around her face. "It's Pat," she says. "Come on. We've got to go."

"Grammy? What's wrong with her?" I hop out of bed and over Sofia's sleeping bag to grab my shoes. Sofia already has her shoes on. She stands up next to me.

"She's missing," says Mom. "Her home care helper came to her house today and she's gone. Car in the garage. Door wide open. They haven't found her yet."

My feet grow roots straight into the ground. "She's gone?"

"She can't have gotten too far. Not too far," says Mom, rushing out of the room.

My breath catches in my throat. Grammy is Dad's mom. We haven't seen her in almost a year. And the last time we did, there was a big fight. Then Dad's depression got really bad and . . . now she's missing?

Sofia squeezes my right hand. The corners of her mouth turn up in a smile, but her eyes stay sad because she knows. She knows I'm scared. "It's going to be okay," she says. She touches her cross necklace. "I'll say a prayer."

I swallow the lump of something hard in my throat and nod. I still don't know what I think of God and praying, but I know Sofia believes it helps. "Thanks."

We walk to the car, hand in hand.

Sofia and I have been best friends since first grade when Adam Shuler pushed her into a mud puddle and I pushed him back. Standing next to her is like looking out my bedroom window when the sun is setting over the almond orchard and smelling the almost-night air.

On the way to Sofia's house, Mom's cell phone rings. She answers it. "Hello . . . oh, thank goodness . . . yes . . . yes . . . I'm on my way . . . I understand . . . thank you . . . bye." Mom pulls the car to the side of the road and sits there with her hands on the steering wheel for a second.

"Mom?"

She grabs the back of the passenger seat and turns around. "They found her."

I lean my head against the back of the seat, the seatbelt pushing against my ear.

"Is she okay?" asks Sofia. "Is she hurt?"

"Well, she's . . . confused."

"Confused?" I ask.

Mom nods. "I think . . . I don't think she can live on her own anymore. Her home care helper told me a few months ago that she was seeming more forgetful. But your dad had just left . . ." Her voice trails off, the silence bringing back more memories than words ever could. "I was too upset to do much about it besides up the frequency of visits from her helper. And now . . . this is all my fault."

"It's not your fault, Mrs. Mitchell," Sofia pipes up.

"Thanks, sweetie." Mom looks at me. "Kate, I think she's really sick."

My heart is still beating fast as if I've just raced Sofia through the almond orchard. "Sick how?"

"Sick in her brain."

I pull my knees up to my chest and hug them against the seat belt. "Like Dad?"

Mom unclicks her buckle so she can turn all the way around. "Not exactly. Your dad has depression. But Grammy, I think she has what's called dementia. It makes old people forget things. I'm . . ." Mom pauses. "I'm going to invite her to live with us. We can take care of her here."

I bite the inside of my cheek, and my stomach buzzes like

a guitar chord played just a little bit off. When I was little, we visited Grammy all the time. I would have loved her to come live with us. But if she's forgetting things, what if she's not the same Grammy? Then again, I don't want her to be the same Grammy as last time we saw her, when she was so angry and mean. I don't want *that* Grammy in our house.

"She's going to need help, Kate," Mom continues. "Help with . . . well, with everything."

"Everything," I whisper. The word gets bigger, so full of questions it might pop. It presses against all of us, pushing us apart. It seeps into the spaces between Sofia and me. It crowds out the sound of the birds chirping. The word *everything* changes things.

Mom turns around and puts the car into drive. Her eyes glance at me in the rearview mirror as she clears her throat. "Thanks for coming to sleep over last night, Sofia. I'm sorry it had to end early."

"It's okay," Sofia says. But she's looking at me when she says it. "It's going to be okay."

I look away because I don't believe her.

# Chapter 4

*A*fter we drop off Sofia, it's a long two-hour drive to Sacramento. Mom keeps getting phone calls. She answers with *hmms* and *yeses* and *okays*. I don't say anything. Grammy's *everything* is still pushing up against me. I wish I could give it a good side kick and shatter it into tiny pieces.

As Mom drives, I find myself humming "Alley Cat," the jazz song Grammy used to play all the time when I was little. I'd march around the living room banging a pot with a spoon. Every time the song was over, Grammy would laugh and say, "That's what I want played at my funeral." I wish Grammy could have just stayed like that.

Finally, we make it to her house. It looks the same. Lace curtains in the window. Rosebushes in the yard, though nobody seems to have pruned them in a while. Mom takes my hand when I get out of the car.

"I don't know what she's going to be like when we walk in," says Mom. "She might not seem like herself. Don't be scared."

I'm not scared. Not at all. But I know Mom must be because she needs to talk through her feelings. Dad used to say she was a patient and therapist all rolled up into one person.

*"And I'm a dang good therapist," she'd reply.*

*"And a good patient," Dad said, nudging her with his elbow. "Very regular appointments."*

"You ready, Katydid?" Mom asks.

I wiggle my hand away. Whenever Mom calls me Katydid, it's like trying to wear a pair of last year's tennis shoes—something I used to love that pinches and doesn't fit anymore. It's been my special nickname ever since I was a baby and seven weeks premature. Mom and Dad said I was small as a bug. A katydid. But I'm not small as a bug now. And Dad's not here to watch me grow.

"I'm ready."

The home care helper, Margaret, opens the door for us. She's got on blue jeans and a red polo shirt; she leans in to Mom and says, "She's ornery this morning."

"Good to know," Mom whispers back.

When we walk in, there's a clattering of pots and pans from the kitchen. "Who's that? Who's there?" Grammy calls.

She comes around the corner, her white hair frizzy around her ears. "Kate? Can it be? Come give me a hug!"

I look at Mom and she nods, so I creep up to Grammy and put my arms around her. She pulls me into her fluffy chest so I can smell the cinnamon and lemon soap on her dress. Before letting go she says, "I was beginning to wonder if you'd forgotten all about me."

Mom's mouth falls open for a second. She does that a lot when we're around Grammy. "I . . . am . . . so sorry, Pat. It's been . . . well, it's been a really hard year for us."

Grammy straightens up. "Where's my Tony? He didn't come with you?"

"No, Pat. He's, ummm, well, he's . . ."

"Late?" Grammy shakes her head. "As usual. That boy. You know, I didn't raise him that way. I raised him to be on time. Not just on time. Early! We were always early. For church, for school, for parties. But now . . ." Grammy looks into the distance for a few seconds. Everyone leans in, waiting for her to finish. I tug on her dress a little and she blinks a few times, clears her throat. "What was I talking about?"

"Being on time," I whisper.

Grammy laughs. "Being on time? My goodness, I haven't been on time for anything in ages. You know, I think my clock's broken. That must be it. Darn clock."

Mom follows Grammy to a couch in the living room. Margaret says goodbye and we all just sit there. We sit there for so long that I wonder if the dust that coats everything in here will start growing on us as well.

Finally, Mom clears her throat. "Pat, we need to talk about what happened this morning."

Grammy waves her hand in the air. "Pish posh. I went on a morning walk. You know how I like my fresh air. And I got a little turned around because of the fog. It could happen to anyone."

"Margaret says you've been leaving the gas stove on all day."

"Well, she's not complaining about the soup I make for her."

I pull my knees up to my chest.

Mom pushes her hands together and then pulls them

22

apart. Together. Apart. Together. Apart. A slow, silent clap. "She says you shouldn't be living on your own anymore."

"Well, that's a load of codswallop. I've been living on my own all my life. I raised my Tony all by myself after his dad died in Vietnam. I am not about to leave this house with my whole life sitting inside it just because some busybody named Margaret, who comes over here every day like she owns the place, thinks she can kick me out."

I bury my face in my knees, trying to block out the anger echoing off the walls.

"It isn't like that," says Mom.

"Of course it is," Grammy goes on. "I bet she wants my house. Hoping for a good deal on it. I've seen the way she looks at my pool."

"Pat, she's worried about you. I'm worried about you. We just want to help."

"Well, then you can leave! That would help!"

In my mind, I hear the memory of her door slamming. "Don't say that again, Grammy," I whisper. But nobody hears me.

Mom stands up in her I'm-the-boss pose. "Family is family, Pat. We're not leaving you here by yourself."

The room goes silent after that. Mom's statement sucked every single vibration out of it. Grammy shakes her head, slowly stands up, and shuffles into the kitchen without saying a word.

I trace my finger around the flowers on the throw pillow, but it doesn't help me let go of the feeling that I'm a teakettle about to whistle. "Will she ever want to live with us? Without Dad?"

Mom sighs. "I don't think she has much of a choice at this point. It's not like she can go live with him."

"Because we don't know where he is," I whisper, finishing the sentence Mom has been telling me every time I think of another way to help Dad get better and want to come home.

"And other reasons," Mom murmurs.

We sit in the living room and nobody says anything. Grammy's gone back to washing dishes and sweeping all the floors in the house. She won't let anyone help her. We get takeout for dinner even though Grammy insists she can cook. Mom and I sit in that room some more after dinner while Grammy makes a big show of reading her mail in the kitchen. But after a while, she stops shuffling papers and walks back into the living room. She looks down at the floor the same way I do when I know I'm in big trouble. "Elizabeth, can you play 'Can't Help Falling in Love with You?'"

Mom looks up from the *Reader's Digest* she's been thumbing through. "Yes, I think so."

"Can't Help Falling in Love with You" was Grammy and Grandpa's wedding song. And even though Grandpa died in Vietnam, Grammy used to play it, and we'd all sing every time we visited. Well, until the last time, when everything exploded.

"Would you play it for me?" Grammy asked. "I . . . I can't."

"Of course." Mom moves to the piano in the corner of the room faster than a bumblebee moving through Mr. Harris's orchard. She opens it up, carefully wipes the dust off the keys, sets her fingers down, and begins to plunk out the first few arpeggios.

My fingers push down like there are guitar strings under them, because there usually are. I know the chords to this song by heart. But I keep my eyes on Grammy, waiting to see what she'll do. Waiting to see if she'll start shaking again, slam the lid of the piano down, and stomp out, yelling about how she never wants to play that song ever again.

But that doesn't happen. Mom starts singing. Her voice is a little stiff, but the notes brush some dust out of the house and bring back the sparkle I remember.

Grammy sits down in her chair. She closes her eyes, leans back her head, and hums along.

Then something starts filling up inside me, a warm rising and building right in my chest. And for just a moment, I think that maybe I could sing. Right here. Maybe it wouldn't hurt so bad to make music without Dad.

But then Mom plays the very last note. That sparkle shimmers in the air until Grammy opens her eyes, and somehow they seem sharper, like Grammy finally knows what's going on. "Well, I guess we'd better start packing."

# Chapter 5

*Dear Dad,*

*Grammy lives with us now. She sleeps in your office. I still think of it as your office, not her bedroom. She walks around the house every day and asks for you.*

*Remember how you used to write obituaries in your office? I'd sit in the beanbag chair and read. You told me that people lead such interesting lives and you felt honored to write the last memories of them.*

*Your office is still full of memories, both old and new. I think you'd still like it. At least I hope you would.*

*Love,*
*Kate*

# Chapter 6

*T*he second I walk into karate, I feel like a breeze blowing through the orchard, light and sweet.

"Kate," says Mr. Amori with a bow of his head. "Nice to see you again. We missed you."

"It's nice to be back."

Mom hands Mr. Amori a straw and a large cup filled with diet soda.

He quickly puts in the straw and takes a sip. "And I missed you, too, Ms. Mitchell."

"It's straight from the drive-thru."

He takes another sip. "You know, I really owe you a discount."

"Nope," says Mom. She holds up her own soda. "I understand the addiction. I'm just sorry we left you without one for so long."

It's been three weeks since I went to karate. It's been three weeks since I went anywhere except school and Grammy's house. After Grammy said she'd come live with Mom and me, there was a lot to do. Packing up all her things, throwing out the stuff she didn't need anymore, doctor's appointments, meeting with realtors and bankers. Mom did as much as she could during the week, while I was at school. But we hopped in the car every Friday and drove to Sacramento to do everything else. That meant missing karate. And sleepovers with Sofia—not that she seemed to really care. Not since play practice started.

"I didn't miss too much, did I?"

"You'll catch up just fine," says Mr. Amori, with a wink. "Don't worry."

I take my usual place, tightening the brown belt around my waist. I shake my arms and legs. Stretch my neck from side to side. Look around the room. Mom and Grammy take seats in chairs along the back wall. Mom gives me a thumbs up. Grammy pulls some knitting needles from her big gold bag.

"Hey, Kate. You're back!"

I turn around and see Parker Harris. He's got a brown belt, too, just like me. That's what happens when your moms are friends and decide to put their kids in the same activity at the same time. "Hi, Parker."

"My mom said maybe you quit karate, but I knew that couldn't be true. You'd never quit."

"Never." I jog in place for a second or two. "I have to beat you next time we spar."

Parker laughs. "Yeah, right." Then he leans in close to my ear. So close the little hairs on the back of my neck tingle and stand up. "Guess what."

"What?"

"I'm starting school on Monday!" Parker's grin is huge.

I stop moving. "What? No way."

"Yep. Mom's having such a hard time with the new baby, she said she didn't feel like she could do a good job with my homeschooling this year. So . . . I'm going to be in your class! Miss Reynolds, right?"

"Right," I say. It comes out as a squeak. Parker and I have been friends pretty much since we were born. His dad is Mr. Harris, who owns the almond orchard next to our house. We used to play together every day. But then we turned five and I started kindergarten and Parker's mom decided to homeschool him. My mom went back to work, and we didn't see each other quite as much. Only once or twice a week.

That's when Parker's mom and my mom decided to put us both in the same karate class. We've basically grown up kicking and blocking and chopping each other.

Something happened about a month before Dad left, though. Parker walked into the dojo and my tongue turned to sandpaper. My hands get sweaty whenever he's around now, and I say really stupid things that I think about the rest of the night. See, Parker's smart and funny and nice, and I think my heart finally realized it.

All of that was okay when it was just karate and Parker was my secret friend that nobody else knew about. But I'm not sure what to think of him being in my class. Will everybody notice my sweaty hands? What if Sofia doesn't like him? Or worse, what if she does?

I try to act like it's no big deal. Maybe if I pretend, my brain will start to believe it. "Well, I hope you get to sit by me."

"Me too! That would be awesome!"

Mr. Amori always says we should know ourselves. But right now, I have no idea what to think or feel. I'm just a mixed-up blob of happy, nervous, sandpapery goo.

Fortunately, I don't have to say anything else to Parker because Mr. Amori—Sensei—takes a final sip of his soda, walks to the front of the room, and starts taking us through warm-ups. And finally, finally, I get to relax.

The past three weeks with Grammy have felt like running a mile in a heat wave. I wasn't sure how much more I could take of boxes and sorting and taping and markers. I wasn't sure how much more Grammy could take of it either. She'd constantly forget what we were doing and bark, "What are you doing with my things? What do you want with that? That's mine!"

It's been even worse since Sunday, when she officially moved in with us. On good days, she snaps at Mom for asking her questions, then feels bad and tries to help, which is usually a disaster. On bad days, she wanders the house crying and asking if she can go home now.

It makes my chest feel tight and prickly. I haven't had Sofia to help me feel better like usual, either. She tried out for *Annie* and got a pretty big part. Pepper. It didn't feel right to talk about Grammy at school where anyone else could hear us. When I tried calling her a couple times in the evenings, she was never there or was on her way out the door. And of course, no sleepovers. Not even tonight when I'm actually home. Sofia didn't explain why. She just said she couldn't come.

But being at karate feels like being spattered by water droplets from a waterfall on the Mist Trail. Like tiny air conditioners are hitting your skin and making the can't-go-one-more-step tiredness fade away.

I relax into the kata and let the smoothness of each move melt into the next. I can see Parker out of the corner of my eye. He glances at me. Then looks away.

There is no *everything* here. No Mom sighing and stomping down the hall. No emptiness and missing. Sometimes, when things around me keep spinning, spinning, spinning, karate is at the very center, the one place where I can stand still.

When the kata is finished, Sensei says, "We will now practice your jumping side kicks."

They must have learned that while I was gone.

"These are tricky," Sensei continues. He catches my eye and nods. "Do not worry if you're struggling with it. You'll have plenty of time to perfect this move. Remember, effort is better than speed. Quality in performance is a result of quantity in practice. Let's begin."

Sensei demonstrates the move for us, which is exactly like it sounds. A kick to the side while jumping. This isn't just any karate move, though. It's one of the ones they always show in movies. It's the kick I've been waiting years to learn.

Parker and the rest of the class begin jumping and side-kicking. I try to join in, but my kick is wobbly in the air. Parker's is way better than mine.

Sensei walks around the room, coaching each person and having us practice kicking a target. I'm one of the last people he comes to. By the time he gets to me, my thighs are burning and my stomach aches. He holds up the black kicking pad and says, "Okay, Kate. Show me what you've got."

But the target is too high, and I don't think I can even jump two inches off the ground right now. I lean over to take some deep breaths.

Parker has stopped practicing and is watching me. Now my cheeks are burning too.

Sensei slaps the kicking pad. "You can do it." He lowers his voice, and I know that one of his bits of wisdom is coming. "Do not focus on the pain. Focus only on the next move."

Sometimes I think that Sensei knows everything. About karate. About life. About me. I close my eyes, block the ache of my legs, and jump.

# Chapter 7

*A*fter karate, Mom walks up to me and says, "How about ice cream with Parker?"

I'm old enough to know this really means, *I need to have a grown-up conversation with Parker's mom.*

Usually, I'd be super excited. Today though, I can't help having sandpaper tongue and sweaty hands. Plus the wondering about what having Parker in class will be like. These things smash together in my brain.

So I shrug. "Okay."

"Is something wrong?" Mom asks. "Are you tired?"

"No, I'm fine."

She cups her hand around my face and pinches her lips together. That's what Mom always does when she's thinking hard. Finally, her face unpinches. "Okay, let's go. But I want you in bed early tonight. Remember what Mr. Amori said about sleep."

I picture Sensei standing at the front of the dojo with his fist resting in the palm of his other hand. "Every hour of sleep before midnight is worth three hours after."

"That's right," says Mom.

We walk down the street to the ice-cream shop. My mom says this used to be the downtown area where everything happened. It was filled up with tiny shops that only sold one or two things. Books, vacuums, repairs, stuff like that. But then the Air Force base was closed and half the town with it. Now this street feels kind of like my house: empty, with memories of how things used to be—and even those are slipping away.

The bell rings when we all walk into the ice-cream store. Grammy strides straight up to the counter and taps her chin. "Well, I'll be. I forgot how many flavors of ice cream there were. I swear there weren't this many when I was a girl."

The boy behind the counter smiles. "We like to come up with new flavors every month or two."

It's true. At this ice-cream shop the flavors change with the seasons. You never know quite what you're going to get. Dad and I used to come here every Saturday to try a different scoop. My favorite was boysenberry vanilla cheesecake, made with the boysenberries growing just down the road. It stained both my and Dad's lips dark purple. Dad said I might as well finish off the look and let me paint his nails that day, too.

I look for boysenberry ice cream again, but it's not in season.

"Well, my goodness," says Grammy. "I guess I'll have chocolate."

"Grammy, that's boring."

"Boring? Pish posh. At my age, boring is good. Surprises cause heart attacks. Remember that when April Fools' Day rolls around."

Parker laughs, and a little bit of tightness lets go inside me. I don't know how much Parker knows about Grammy, but I'm glad he gets to see her being regular old Grammy tonight, not the Grammy who forgets where she is.

He steps up to the counter and says, "I'll have blood orange mango tango, please."

"Good choice," says the boy behind the counter. "And how about you?" he asks me.

I look at all the different flavors one more time. "I'll take the same thing."

"Hey, good choice." Parker nudges me, and a burst of fireworks erupts from the tiny place between my ribs where his elbow touched.

I turn away to grab my ice cream so he won't see my face heat up.

We all sit at the booth next to the big window at the front. Mom talks to Mrs. Harris. It's the first time I've seen her without the baby, Amelie, since she was pregnant. Grammy doesn't talk to anyone, just eats each bite of her chocolate ice cream as slowly as possible. Parker and I compare karate techniques and our plans for which weapons we'll train with after black belt.

Then, when I'm halfway done with my ice cream, I see Sofia walking past the window with Marisa Nunez. Sofia's carrying her backpack and her green sleeping bag, the one she always brings to my house for sleepovers.

Marisa says something. Sofia laughs. They don't see me.

I watch them cross the street and open the big, dark theater doors.

"Is something wrong?" Parker asks.

Grammy looks up from her chocolate ice cream.

Slowly, I turn away from the window. "Oh, nothing. I saw Sofia with Marisa."

"Sofia, your best friend?"

"Yep."

"Who's Marisa?"

I poke at my ice cream with a spoon. "You'll meet her on Monday."

There's nothing wrong with Marisa Nunez. Not really. She's tall and pretty and lives in a big house, and all the teachers like her. Sofia's been going to church with her for about a year. But Marisa's best friend moved away right before Christmas break and now . . . that sleeping bag.

Grammy leans close to me and whispers, "That used to be you, didn't it?"

I don't say anything, but Grammy nods like she knows everything and never puts yarn in the freezer. "Mmhmm, I've seen that look before. I've been there."

"You have?" I whisper back. "What did you do?"

She puts her lips right close to my ear and says, "Magic."

I sigh and swirl my ice cream around. I guess I couldn't expect Grammy to stay normal all evening.

♪ ♪ ♪

That night, I call Sofia to ask about her rehearsal. Maybe the sleeping bag was a prop for the show. Maybe the theater floor is hard and dirty and Sofia wanted something to sit on.

Her mom answers the phone. "Hello?"

"Hi, Mrs. Martinez. Is Sofia there?"

She clucks. "Oh, I'm sorry, Kate. She's sleeping over at Marisa's tonight."

"Really? But I thought . . ." My voice trails off before I say, *I thought she couldn't sleep over tonight*, because I can't believe I was too stupid to realize what was going on.

"I'll tell her you called, okay?"

After I hang up the phone, my fingers itch for something to do. Something to distract me from thinking about Sofia and Marisa having a sleepover. I walk into the music room and go straight to Dad's guitar.

He left it here when he took off. That's how I know he's coming back. Dad would never leave his guitar forever. He loves it too much. I'd rather think about that right now.

I take the guitar to my bedroom, wipe away the dust, and carefully tune the strings. He'll want to know I took care of it while he was away. I remember what he said.

*"Cradle it. A guitar is like a lover."*

*"Tony!" Mom smacked him lightly on the shoulder. "A lover?"*

*Dad smirked. "Sorry. A guitar is like a baby. Don't hold it stiff. Relax into it."*

I fold toward the guitar and press my fingers against two of the frets. With a small sigh, I gently run my right thumb over all the strings to play an E-minor chord. That's the chord Dad always said was his favorite.

*"An easy way to add a little bit of sadness to a song."*

*"Why would anyone want to add sadness to a song?" I asked.*

*He poked my stomach. "Because if it's in a song, it's not inside you anymore. See?"*

I strum that chord a couple more times, but it doesn't get the sadness out of me. Instead, my eyes get hot, and I have to hurry to put the guitar away.

I'm a brown belt in karate. I don't wear pink. I'm strong.

And crying isn't strong.

That's why I can't make music anymore.
I haven't been able to for a long time.

*Dear Dad,*

*Have you ever had a question but you were afraid of the answer? I have a question for Sofia but I'm scared to ask it.*

*I have lots of questions for you too. Questions like when will you come home? Why did you leave us? Do you still love me?*

*But I wouldn't ask those things even if I could. Because what if the answers are never, you did something wrong, and no?*

*Love,*
*Kate*

# Chapter 8

*T*he next Monday is February fifth. Spring is here. The blossoms on the trees in Mr. Harris's orchard this morning prove it.

Spring hasn't changed Miss Reynolds's class any, though. She still stands so straight and tall you'd think she had a ruler glued to her back, but she holds her hands the way a princess would and swishes from place to place, as if she's wearing a ball gown and not a flannel skirt and sweater. Right now she's reading something. A poem, I think.

It's actually probably a great poem. Miss Reynolds only reads us really good stuff, but I'm not hearing any of it. Because I can't stop staring at the hugest cherry-blossom–colored ribbon ever. It's on Sofia's head, right over her long, brown ponytail. My stomach buzzes like there's a bunch of honeybees inside itching to fly out.

One measly sleepover and Sofia goes back on our pinkie promise and decides to become Pink One and Pink Two with Marisa? I tap my pencil against my desk. At least Sofia isn't wearing *all* pink, though. It's just the bow in her hair. Marisa is way worse. Her entire outfit is a bright shade of bubblegum. Hideous.

My eraser rubs a hole through my paper. I tried to call Sofia yesterday. I wanted to tell her about how Grammy forgot who I was that morning. My hair was pulled back under a baseball cap and she looked at me and said, "Tony!" It always hurts when she says Dad's name. Having her see him when she looks at me is a new kind of sting, though.

But when I called, Sofia wasn't home from church yet, and she must have been busy afterwards because she didn't call me back.

I didn't think big and important things like best friends could change so quickly. Then again, all it takes is one day for Mr. Harris to put out his bee boxes and suddenly winter is gone.

I stare at that pink bow, pull out one of my special sparkly gel pens, and put it to a new, fresh, hole-less piece of notebook paper.

*Sofia*, I write. I'm not sure what to say next. Some words, like *Why did you break your promise?* should only be spoken, not written. They're the kind of words that you hope can disappear after you say them. I think for a moment and then write our code for *we need to talk.*

*Sofia,*
*Penguins balance eggs on their feet. Lockers, after lunch.*
*Kate*

I tap my pen on the paper a few times. When I look up again, I'm practically blinded by Marisa's bubblegum sweatshirt and pants. And I know it's not nice, but I can't help writing something to show Sofia how silly she looks.

*P.S. Don't you think Marisa looks exactly like a stick of gum today?*

One of Sensei's favorite sayings rings in my head. *Kindness is the greatest form of strength.* But Sensei's words are easier to ignore than those bees in my stomach.

I sloppily fold the note into a small square, nothing fancy. I never can figure out that fancy note folding. After I write *Sofia* on top, I tap Amy's shoulder in front of me. She takes the note in this sneaky way where she pretends to scratch her shoulder, but is really grabbing the paper, and then slowly moves her hand up to the front of her desk and nudges Alejandro, who taps Sofia's elbow with the note.

Sofia isn't as sneaky as Amy; she just turns around and grabs it. That gets Marisa's attention.

*Oh, no.*

She won't understand the coded message, but thinking about Marisa reading the P.S. on that note makes me want to crawl over the tops of the desks and snatch it away.

Marisa leans way over to see who sent the note. When she sees *Sofia* written in my special sparkly ink, she turns and looks at me for a second like she just realized I existed and might still want my best friend. Marisa whispers something to Sofia.

Sofia shakes her head, but Marisa whispers something else.

Sofia told me once that Marisa tells her to do things she

doesn't want to do and that she has a hard time saying no. It didn't seem like a big deal before, when it only happened at church. But now I may as well be in one of those courtroom shows, waiting for the judge to give me a verdict.

Sofia's shoulders slump forward. She turns the note over, unfolds it, and lets Marisa read it right alongside her.

My fingers clench the edge of my desk, and I suck in my breath. She's just like Benedict Arnold. I only know that because Miss Reynolds taught us about him this morning, but I didn't think Sofia would ever, ever in a million years act like him. I never thought she'd betray me.

I can tell the minute Marisa finishes reading. Her back stiffens, and she pulls off her bright pink jacket. Underneath it is a sparkly pink shirt though, which isn't much better. Marisa seems to realize this. She crosses her arms over her chest and spreads her hands out over her sleeves.

"Miss Reynolds," she says.

*No.*

"Someone is passing Sofia notes, and it's distracting me."

Miss Reynolds stops reading, makes a humming noise, and plucks that note out of Sofia's grasp. The little hairs on my arm stand up.

Miss Reynolds's slender hands barely touch the note, holding it like it's been made by the sweet mice and birds who sew her flannel skirts at night and might fall apart at any second. Her eyes find me. "Kate," she says, "what do you have to say to me for interrupting my class?"

"I'm sorry."

"And to Marisa and Sofia for distracting them?"

I slide down low in my chair trying to hide. "Sorry."

Miss Reynolds nods to Marisa and Sofia. "You were

obviously riveted by the words of George Ella Lyon. Perhaps you'd like to finish reading the poem to the class?"

Marisa raises her hand. "I would!" She never gives up a chance to perform.

"Go ahead," Miss Reynolds hands her the book.

Marisa takes a deep breath and speaks in her stage voice. All her words turn to mush in my brain, though.

Sofia showed Marisa my note. A special, secret, just-between-friends thing. If she shared that with Marisa, what else has she shared with her? That I'm afraid of caterpillars? How I peed my pants on the Ferris wheel? That my dad left and never came back? I don't know what I can trust her to keep secret anymore.

I try to stare Sofia down. Try to make her turn around and see me with just the force of my eyeballs. But she doesn't move.

I drum my fingers on the desk a few times before Parker leans over. As he turns the page of the book he's sneakily reading in his lap—*The Hobbit*—he whispers, "Hey, it's okay. You don't need to be so nervous."

My face heats up. Just like he promised on Friday, Parker's in my class, and Miss Reynolds sat him right next to me. He's been reading all morning, though, even telling me, "You don't pause when Bilbo's facing trolls" when I asked if he was going to put the book away for Language Arts.

Do I say something back? Will everyone know I like him if I do? I stop drumming my fingers and instead start twisting my hair.

When Marisa finishes reading, Miss Reynolds clears her throat and rubs the corner of her eye. "Thank you, Marisa. Now class, wasn't that a beautiful poem?"

Nobody says anything. A few people shrug their shoulders.

"Your enthusiasm is overwhelming today." Miss Reynolds claps her hands. "Okay, next I want everyone to partner up!"

I snap to attention, pulling myself out of my chair as quickly as I can. "Sofia," I call.

But before she can turn around, Marisa's arm shoots out and grabs Sofia's shoulder.

Sofia glances back toward me and mouths, "Sorry."

I want to tell her it's okay, that I know we're still best friends so it doesn't matter. Instead, I flop back into my chair and turn to where Parker was sitting only a few seconds before, but he's gone, paired up with someone else across the room.

"I'll be your partner," says a voice. It's Jane Chu. She stands next to my desk and leans toward me, waiting for an answer.

"Oh, um . . ." I glance back at Sofia again. I don't know why. Maybe I'm hoping she'll change her mind. But she doesn't. She just laughs at something Marisa said and scoots her desk a little closer.

I give Jane a small smile. "Sure."

"Oh good!" Jane throws herself into the desk next to me, her smooth black hair swinging into her face. "Whatever the assignment is, I'm in charge of drawing, okay?"

"Okay," I say with a shrug.

"Unless . . ." Jane kind of points at me with her hand. "I mean, you don't really want to draw, right?"

"Nah."

Sofia is laughing again.

"Oh good," says Jane. "I love to draw. I'm not, like, super great at it. But I'm better than most of the Picassos around here." Jane winks at me and I can't help it, I laugh. Just a small laugh, more a snort, but it's enough to get Sofia to turn around for a second and look. First at me. Then at Jane.

I glance down at Jane's pink tennis shoe and orange tennis shoe. Jane moved to Atwater last summer, and I don't know much about her except that she tries to wear as many colors as she possibly can all at once. Some people think that's weird. I guess everyone likes a rainbow, but not really on a person. Part of me wonders what Sofia will think of me and Jane being partners.

Miss Reynolds claps her hands again to get everybody's attention. "Here is your assignment. Write a 'Where I'm From' poem like the one we just read, but for yourself. Remember to write lines that put us in the places you have been and show us the things you've experienced. Make us see, feel, hear, and taste them. You're going to hand your poem off to your partner in a second for the next part of this project. Although . . ." Miss Reynolds looks at the watch on her wrist. "That might have to wait until after lunch. We'll see. Okay. Start writing!"

The whole class gets to work. I turn to Jane and say, "I kind of didn't listen to the poem."

She's sketching the letter K and filling it with flowers. "Yeah, I know," she says without looking up from her notebook. "I figured that out when you were passing notes. It's okay. It's super easy. Here, I'll show you."

She rips out a piece of notebook paper and taps her pencil on it while she squinches her lips up to one side. "Okay, so I'm Chinese, and my grandma loves to cook. I'm an artist and an only child." She writes all of that on the paper. "But that doesn't sound like poetry, right?"

"I guess not."

"You guess?" Jane looks up at me from underneath her thick black bangs. "Have you ever listened to poetry?"

I think back to Dad one night with his guitar in his arms, writing me a song on the spot.

*"How do you do that, Daddy?"*

*He stopped strumming. "How do I do what?"*

*"Make up the words like that? How do you know what to say?"*

*Dad laughed, reached out, and tweaked my nose. "A song is just a poem. And a poem is just words with enough space in between them for your heart to take a deep breath and keep going."*

"I've listened to poetry," I tell Jane. "Lots of it."

Jane smiles. "Good. Then you'll be awesome at this. So now, all I have to do is look at that list of details about me and where I come from and make them more poemy."

"How do you do that?"

Jane hunches over and whispers like it's a secret. "You close your eyes and think about how all those things feel on your skin and in your ears and on your tongue, and you write it down."

The hair on my neck stands up the way it does whenever Dad plays a key change.

Jane and I both get to work, and by the time I'm done, my brain feels looped around my pencil. But I've got a poem. At least, it looks like a poem.

*I am from the gravel just beyond*
*The last almond tree in the orchard.*
*From air whistling when my leg*
*Slices through it in a perfect kick.*
*I'm from the slow build of piano chords,*

*Guitar strings, and a trio of voices*
*Chasing away emptiness.*

My pencil hovers over that last line wanting to erase something from so deep inside me off that paper and away from the eyes of people I barely know.

Sofia laughs, and I lose my concentration. She and Marisa lean their heads close, giggling about something. Marisa glances at me and then looks away.

I feel like I'm on the other side of a window with my nose pressed up against the glass. What are they saying? Why is Sofia laughing? There's only one way to find out. I slowly drop my hand with the pencil to the side of my chair and let the pencil roll down my palm, off my fingers, and onto the floor. It comes to a stop next to Amy's desk.

Close enough.

"Oh, let me—" says Jane, about to stand.

"No," I whisper. "I've got it."

I glance at Sofia and Marisa to make sure their backs are turned and then very casually sidle up to where my pencil lies on the ground.

Amy looks up from her paper, smiles at me, and goes back to writing.

"You don't think this shirt is too pink, right?" I hear Marisa whisper as I crouch down.

Sofia replies. "No. I like it."

"Well, then why did Kate make fun of it?"

I slowly reach for my pencil. Amy looks at me again, her eyebrows furrowed. Right before I grab it, Adam Shuler swings his leg out and kicks it further down the aisle. He snickers, not realizing he's actually helping me listen longer.

"Oh." Sofia sighs as I crawl along the floor toward my pencil. I expect her to explain to Marisa about best friends forever and our pinkie promise. Instead, she says, "That's just something Kate and I used to do. No pink. Kind of silly."

I freeze. I want to hear if Sofia says something else. Anything else to explain and make me feel better. But blood is whooshing through my ears sounding like crashing ocean waves and all I hear is *silly, silly, silly*.

"Okay, class. Time for lunch!" Miss Reynolds calls.

Sofia and Marisa stand up and head out the door. A whole bunch of feet belonging to the rest of the class follow them. I grab my pencil and lean back into a crouch, unable to move under the weight of *silly, silly, silly*.

Then Jane jumps in front of me. "Hey! Whatcha doing?"

With a gasp, I fall against the desk behind me, my head scraping the underside of it. My hair catches on a big, sticky blob of freshly chewed bubblegum.

I scoot out, trying to pull my hair away from the gum, but the gum stretches and follows me, forming a long, slimy pink bridge from the bottom of the desk to my head.

"Yuck!" I stand up, pinch the gum with two fingers, and try to pluck it out, but that only makes things worse—the gum smears in my hair from right above my ear to my jawline. "Oh, gross. What am I going to do?"

"Uh-oh," says Jane.

"Everything okay over there, girls?" Miss Reynolds calls from the door.

"Yes," I say.

"Okay, well, let's get going."

I put my hand over the gum in my hair, and Jane and I walk out to the hallway and our lockers. When we get out there, Miss Reynolds is talking with another teacher. Jane stands on her tiptoes. "Let me see that." She pokes at the pink goo. "Ugh, freshly chewed. That's stuck good. Sorry."

"It's not your fault," I mumble. "I shouldn't have been on the floor." I really shouldn't have. The word *silly* starts echoing in my brain again.

Jane sticks a hand on her hip. "Nice try. It's totally my fault! If I hadn't been a goose and surprised you this never would have happened." She sighs and shakes her head. "I get too excited. Mom says I'm basically a Labrador retriever."

I smile. "I've never seen a rainbow Lab."

Jane's eyes get wide, and for a minute I think maybe I hurt her feelings. But then she starts laughing—this loud laugh that fills up every molecule of air between us with something like warm honey.

"That's a good one," Jane says. "I'm going to tell my mom that next time." We begin trudging down the hallway. "So what are you going to do about . . . that?" She points at my hair.

"Probably call my mom. I can't walk around the rest of the day like this."

"No way," Jane agrees.

When we get to the place where you can either turn left for the cafeteria or right for the office, we both stand there for a minute longer, neither one of us wanting to let go of that warm-honey feeling. Finally, Jane says, "You're funny, Kate. Do you want to come to my house after school? I've got a trampoline, and my mom will make cookies. I haven't really had anyone over to my house since we moved in." She shrugs. "It'll be fun. I promise."

I almost say okay, but then I stop. Being friends isn't quite that easy when you have Grammy at home. If I went over to Jane's house, then I'd have to invite her over to my house next. And if Jane came to my house, she'd meet Grammy. It might be a good day, and Grammy would be fine and make cookies. But it could also be a bad day when she wanders around looking for Dad, or ties her knitting up into big knots and cries.

It's okay if Sofia sees those things, but I'm not ready to share that part of me with Jane. Sometimes school friends are best because you can hide the parts of your life that maybe don't look like you wish they did.

"I can't."

Jane nods her head fast. Too fast. "Oh, that's okay. I figured. Too soon. That's the Labrador retriever again."

She tries to laugh at the joke, but it's stiff, and her smile doesn't reach her eyes. I feel like I've erased one of the stripes on a rainbow. "I have to watch my little sister," I blurt out.

Jane tilts her head to the side. "You have a sister?"

"Yeah." I lean into the lie, let it wrap its fingers around my lungs.

"Lucky," says Jane. "I *wish* I had a sister."

I don't say anything else about it, just point down the hall toward the office. "Well, I better call my mom."

"Okay. See you later," Jane says before walking away.

I watch her rainbow headband bob up and down as she pulls a piece of paper from her pocket and disappears around the corner.

# Chapter 9

*T*he secretary, Miss Williams, looks up from her computer as I open the door. "May I help you?"

"I need to use the phone." I point to my hair.

"Uh-oh," she says before pushing the old black thing in my direction. "Here you go."

"Thanks." The clock on the wall shows that it isn't one yet, so Mom might still be at home having lunch with Grammy. I call the house phone first.

It only rings once before Grammy answers. "Mitchell residence."

"Hi, Grammy," I say. "Is Mom there?"

"Oh, is this Kate? What are you doing calling from school?" She gasps. "Is everything okay? Are you hurt? Are you sick?"

"No, I'm fine. I got gum stuck in my hair. I need Mom to come get me."

Grammy clicks her tongue. "Gum in the hair. That is a problem. Hmmmm. Your mother's not here. Maybe I could . . . where did you say you were again, Kate?"

I look at all the walls, searching for an answer. "Oh, um, nowhere. I'm nowhere."

"Nowhere," she squawks. "How can you be nowhere? That's just silly. Now I'll tell you what—"

"No," I cut in. "It's okay. I'm fine really. The gum's already out of my hair. Look at that."

Miss Williams looks at me funny from her black leather seat and raises an eyebrow. I don't know how to tell her that Grammy has her helpful voice on. And when Grammy has her helpful voice on, she wants to repay Mom and me for everything, and soon we end up with burnt cookies, bleach-stained laundry, and a garden overflowing with water because she forgot to turn the hose off. If she tries to come to school, she might get lost.

"Are you sure?" asks Grammy. "You know I've got nothing to do here but the crossword puzzle, and heaven knows I haven't been able to finish one of them in years."

"I'm sure." I hold my breath and wait for her to believe me.

"Okay, then. What's a ten-letter word for stubborn?"

"I don't know."

Grammy grumbles. "Well, then why are you calling me? Good heavens, child." And she hangs up the phone.

I let out a sigh of relief and hang up the phone for a few seconds before calling again—this time Mom's cell phone.

"Hello?" She answers.

"Hi, Mom."

"Is everything okay, Katydid?"

"It's just Kate," I say. "I'm too old for Katydid."

Someone speaks in the background. Mom talks back, her voice muffled because she's trying to cover up the phone. "Just get those to *mmmf-fum-fum*." Then she's back to me. "Katydid, did you need something?"

I sigh and talk a little louder. "Yeah, I got gum in my hair."

"How? You're not supposed to be chewing gum. Especially not in school."

"It wasn't me. I didn't chew it. It was . . . someone else."

Another voice in the background. "Katydid," Mom says. She sounds like she's running. "I've got a big presentation today, and I'm already running late for it. I'm sorry. We'll get the gum out of your hair when you get home, all right?"

She's about to hang up, the way she always does when she's super busy at work, when she says goodbye but doesn't wait for me to say it back. I yell as quick as I can, "What about Dad?"

That stops her fast. Talking about Dad always does. "What about him?"

"Could I . . . could I call him? Do you think he could come get me?"

Mom sighs. I know she's making that face she always makes when I talk about Dad. The one where everything pulls down—her mouth, her eyes, the lines around her nose, even her ears get lower. "Katydid, you know what will happen."

"Maybe not this time."

"Maybe."

"I'm going to try. Okay, Mom?"

"Okay, honey." Papers crinkle into the phone. "Katydid?"

"Yeah?"

"Don't get your hopes up okay?"

I hang up without saying anything, then quickly lift the phone again and call Dad, slowly punching my finger into each number. I know it's not true, but I can't help thinking that maybe this time, if I do it just right, he'll answer. Once I've called, I count the rings until I reach his voicemail.

"This is Anthony Mitchell."

Listening to Dad's voicemail has become a bit of a ritual. I close my eyes. Imagine the way the corners of his mouth twist up when he says, "Sorry I missed your call, but go ahead and leave a message so I can get back to you."

Mom was right. Again. I sigh and draw invisible figure eights on the counter. "Hi, Dad. It's me . . . Kate . . . your daughter. I sort of got gum in my hair at school. It's pink and sticky and I need to go home. Can you come get me? Please? If you get this, just call my school. Okay? It's Atwater Elementary in case you don't remember. Okay, bye."

I hang up the phone soft and quiet, the way I always do when I call him. Like hanging it up too hard might break something.

"Nobody coming?" asks Miss Williams.

I shake my head. "But my dad might call back. If he does—"

"I'll let you know." She stares at the gum. "You know, I have a hat. If you'd like to, you may wear it the rest of the day."

"Really?" I touch that sticky spot in my hair again. "That would be super nice."

Miss Williams winks at me as she reaches underneath her desk. I stand on tiptoe, leaning over the counter and holding my breath. She pulls out a small, pink knitted hat.

"Oh," I breathe.

The hat hangs from her hand like a wilted flower. "Here you go."

The pink is so awfully soft and helpless looking.

*Silly, silly, silly.*

I pull my hand away from my hair, lift my chin up, and say, "No, thank you. I'm good. Really." And then I walk out the door before Miss Williams can say anything else.

# Chapter 10

$I$t's a long walk to the cafeteria. First, I stop by my locker and grab my lunch. Then I have to pass all the trophy cases and bulletin boards, and my reflection keeps showing up in the glass with that gum sticking out. I've gone five years not ever wearing a stitch of pink. Pink is silly and weak, and that's not me. There's no pink in karate. Now all of a sudden it's stuck on me and there's nothing I can do about it.

When I get to the cafeteria, I peek in the door at all the circular gray tables. I find the one where Sofia and I always sit. But my chair, the chair on Sofia's right, is taken. Marisa is there, slurping her chicken and noodles while crossing her eyes. And Sofia is laughing. Laughing? At something that stupid?

Then I remember the other thing Sofia told Marisa. *That's just something Kate and I used to do.*

Used to. Like we *used to* be best friends.

Jane smiles at me from her table with Brooklyn and Emma, but I take a step backward. And another one. And another one. Until I'm all the way back in the hall. Then I turn, and my feet are taking me away from the cafeteria. Faster and faster. Out of the hall and into the girls' bathroom.

It's empty in here. Thank goodness.

The handle on the sink faucet is cold to the touch. I spin it around. When icy water gushes out, I run my hands underneath. It's like sticking my hands in Mirror Lake right at the beginning of spring when all the snow has melted. Mom and Dad used to take me every year. We'd put our feet in and see who could last the longest. Mom always won. Dad used to joke that she was summoning a hot flash.

*"I'm not that old yet," she laughed and smacked his shoulder.*

*"Almost," he said back.*

*Mom tucked that strip of gray hair behind her ears. "Almost isn't there yet."*

But Dad didn't take me to Mirror Lake this year. He barely left his room all last summer. I turn off the water because the coldness of it hurts too much.

I don't know how long I stay there, hunched over the sink, hair hanging in my face, all tangled up in memories of Dad and thoughts about Sofia sitting at lunch with Marisa, wearing pink like Marisa, laughing at Marisa, letting Marisa read my note. Finally, the bell rings, and the chorus of feet running back to class echoes outside the bathroom door. I wait until everyone's gone before I leave.

When I turn down the hallway to class, Sofia's sitting against the wall of lockers. "Oh, your hair," she says. "What happened?"

I ignore her and walk past, stomping the way Mom does,

hoping Sofia will feel my anger. But I don't get very far before she says, "I've been waiting for you. Lockers. After lunch. What do you want to talk about?"

I stop. My back is to her, but I don't turn around.

I want to say, *I can't believe you let her read it.*

I want to say, *How could you have a sleepover with her instead of me?*

I want to yell and scream and shout and pull that pink ribbon off her head.

But the words that come out of my mouth instead are, "Grammy called me Tony yesterday." My legs are wobbly as I say it and turn around, like they're hoping Sofia can suddenly be strong enough for both of us.

Sofia bites her lip. "She's getting worse, isn't she?"

"Yeah, she is." The words feel as if they're clawing against my throat as they come out.

"Did your dad come home to see her yet?"

"No." I change the subject away from secrets Sofia might not keep. "You should come to my house tonight. It's Chinese-food night. Your favorite."

Sofia stands up. "I wish I could. But I'm going to Marisa's to practice my lines for *Annie*."

"Of course." I pull at the pieces of hair sticking out from my bubblegum catastrophe. "Are you going to paint your nails pink tonight, too?"

The angry words are out before I can stop them. I think of Sensei and how he would say, *The tongue is the most difficult part of the body to control.*

Sofia stares at me, hard and unblinking. "If I want to wear pink, I'll wear pink. That was your stupid rule."

"But you promised," I say, a little too loud.

"It's just a color. It doesn't mean anything!"

All the air whooshes out of my lungs.

Sofia sighs. "Come on. Miss Reynolds will know I'm not actually in the bathroom soon."

For a second, I can't move. I'm like the Tin Man without any oil. It takes Sofia turning around and breezing into the classroom to get my joints working again. I grab the door right before it slams shut and walk into class, too. Miss Reynolds greets me with, "Kate, you're tardy."

"I know," I murmur, robotic.

"Do you have an excuse?"

"No."

Miss Reynolds's eyes catch on the gum and she softens. "Please don't be late again."

"Okay."

I walk past Marisa, who looks at my hair as if there's a hamster living in it, past Sofia, who's straightening out her pens and pencils, and up to Parker, sneakily reading *The Hobbit* in his lap. He doesn't look up. Bilbo must still be in danger. As I sit down, he whispers, "What did Sofia say?"

I freeze. "What?"

"Sofia? Didn't she talk to you out in the hall?"

Sofia turns around and watches me whispering with Parker. I shake my head. "I don't . . . it was nothing." But the prickly poking at the corner of my eyes doesn't feel like nothing.

Parker glances up from his book at the gum in my hair, then back down to *The Hobbit*. I probably look worse than one of those trolls in his book.

"Okay, class," Miss Reynolds calls. "Back to our group projects. It's time to swap poems with your partner."

Jane's on the far side of the room, bent over a piece of

white paper. She stops making broad lines with her pencil just long enough to turn in her seat and give me a little wave. I cover the gum in my hair and walk over.

When I take the seat next to Jane she whispers, "It's okay. It's really only noticeable from, like, certain angles."

"Which ones?"

She squints at me and moves around a bit from side to side. "The front." Pause. "And this side." She moves behind me. "And the back."

I groan.

"But hey! Not from the other side!"

"That's most angles." I put my hand back over the gum.

"I know. I was trying to make you feel better."

I sigh and hand her my poem. She gives me hers, and we both read in silence.

Jane's poem is fantastic. When I read it, I get tingles.

*I am from charcoal, graphite, pastel*
*Smudged onto my fingertips,*
*From tangerine and fuchsia Converse*
*Swapped for rubber tuoxie slippers that I*
*Tap, tap, tap against my grandma's kitchen stool*
*As peppercorns crackle in her wok.*

I peek at Jane to see if she thinks my poem is terrible compared to hers. But her hand is over her mouth and she's squinting like she's really concentrating. I don't know if that's good or bad.

"Now," announces Miss Reynolds. "Pick your favorite part of your partner's poem, circle it, and share it with them."

Jane and I look at each other for a second and giggle. Jane

goes first. "I really liked the part about the music. 'I'm from the slow build of piano chords, guitar strings, and a trio of voices.'"

"I like your line about charcoal and graphite on your fingertips."

"Thanks!"

A few seconds later, Miss Reynolds says, "Did you pick one out and share it? Good. Here comes the fun part. You and your partner together are going to write another one of these poems, but this time for a famous person in history, and then . . ."—she pauses with a finger pointing toward the ceiling and looks around the room—"on Thursday, you will present your poem to the class. But you will not just read your poem. No, no. That's boring." Miss Reynolds laughs. "You're going to present the poem you and your partner write about a famous person in a way that represents those favorite parts from each of your personal poems. You can perform together if that works, or split the poem into two parts and perform separately. Your choice."

The class stares. Miss Reynolds stares back at us, her mouth open in an excited O like she's waiting for us to cheer or something. "So you'll be using something about you to share something about a person from history!"

Again. Silence.

"Here, I'll give you an example." Suddenly, Miss Reynolds is in front of me, whisking my poem away and reading the part Jane circled. "'I'm from the slow build of piano chords, guitar strings, and a trio of voices.' Oh, that is lovely." She holds up my piece of paper. "So, Kate here could sing for her and Jane's presentation."

My heart starts beating super fast. "No," I whisper. But

Miss Reynolds doesn't hear me. She's still talking.

"Presentations will be on Thursday; you'll have the next two days to research, write, and plan together. I can't wait to see what you come up with."

The class begins murmuring, partners leaning their heads together. Jane picks up her poem. "So you'll be singing. Maybe I can . . ."

I shake my head. "No. No way."

"But the poem made it sound like . . . you like to sing?"

I can't help thinking of Mom and Dad and me crowded into the music room, laughing and singing.

*Oh, Shenandoah, I long to hear you.*

I shake my head, and the memory disappears like someone threw a rock through the window.

But before I can say *I don't sing anymore*, Sofia is next to me. "Are you really going to sing?"

I open my mouth but no sound comes out. I want to say yes. If it means Sofia will stand by my desk and talk to me and look at me like she thinks I'm awesome again, I want to sing.

Maybe it's like Sofia said about wishing and praying. *It never hurts to try everything. Not when it's important.* Everything includes things you don't want to do.

"Um, I guess so."

Sofia bounces a little. "Yes! I can't wait." Then a little quieter. "If you're singing again, you can totally do the next musical with me and Marisa."

"Oh, yeah. You and Marisa."

Everything goes blurry except Sofia waving at me and then walking back to Marisa, who gives me a quizzical look.

Suddenly, the intercom buzzes. "Miss Reynolds?" comes Miss Williams's voice.

"Yes?"

"Will you please send Katherine Mitchell to the office?"

"She's on her way."

It's Dad.

It has to be.

He's come to take me home. The blurry brain fog clears immediately. I jump up, grab my poem, and practically skip out of class. Maybe I will be able to sing again. Maybe this is like that moment at the end of a fermata, when you're not sure your voice can hold out much longer, but then finally, you get to breathe and the music moves forward again.

# Chapter 11

*I* walk through the halls as fast as I can without getting in trouble. Once the office doors are in sight, I search for any sign of Dad—his A's baseball cap with the red stain, anything. But all I see is frizzy white hair, a purple dress, and a big gold bag.

"Grammy," I say as I walk in. The doors that lead to the rest of the school buzz as they lock automatically behind me. "What are you doing here?"

When she turns around, I can tell she's not at the school. Not really. She's lost somewhere inside her brain. Her eyes are wide and she taps the ends of her fingers together. "Kate," she says. "Oh, Kate. Is this the post office? I thought this was the post office, and I have this letter." She opens her gold bag. "It's somewhere in here."

Miss Williams slides a white envelope across the counter. "It's right here, dearie."

I don't like how she says *dearie*. Like Grammy's a child or something. "This is my grandma," I say.

"I was hoping that was the case. Otherwise, I would have had to call the police. She mentioned a phone call from Kate and the name on the letter is Anthony Mitchell. I put two and two together and I'm glad I was right."

Grammy snatches the letter back from Miss Williams. "That is my personal mail. It's very important. I just . . . And she won't mail it!" Grammy points at Miss Williams. "I need to get this letter to Tony. I need to get it to him today!"

I take the letter out of her hand and look at the name written across the top of it in big curvy letters.

*Anthony Mitchell.*

Dad. There's no address underneath. Just empty space and the invisible question: Where is he?

"He needs it," Grammy whispers. "He needs to know I love him."

I run my finger over that spot where an address should be, the spot that should be filled with my address. "It's okay," I say. "I'll make sure he gets it. I promise."

"I don't want you making sure he gets my letter," says Grammy. "This woman should make sure he gets my letter. It's her job. This is a post office after all."

"No, Grammy. You're at my school."

"Oh." Her eyebrows unscrunch and she looks around the office. "Oh. Oh, yes." She takes the letter back. It shakes in her hands. "I . . . I think I need to go home." She stuffs the envelope back into her purse. "I'm so sorry," she says to Miss Williams. "So, so sorry. I can be such a silly old woman sometimes."

"It's quite all right, dear."

Grammy opens the office door to leave.

"Wait!" I walk up to Miss Williams and whisper, "Can I walk her home? Just in case?"

"I'll need to call your mother to get permission."

After Miss Williams hangs up the phone with Mom, she says, "Your mother will meet you at home, Kate."

A few minutes later, Grammy and I are outside. The morning fog has burned away somewhere up in the sky, and the sun shines bright and white. We pass the bus stop where a mom with a baby is waiting. The bus here loops all around the edges of town, which are covered with orchards and farmland, and then turns into the center, where the businesses and stores are, to drop people off at supermarkets and the post office.

"Oh my," Grammy says as we cross the street. "That was embarrassing."

"It's okay. Miss Williams is nice. She doesn't care."

"She treated me like a baby."

"I know. I didn't like that either."

Grammy sighs and puts her arm on my shoulder. It's kind of a hug, but also kind of a help, so she can step over the curb and back onto the sidewalk. We walk by Mr. Harris's almond orchard. The branches are filled with white flowers and his bee boxes are out by the side of the road. When the wind blows, flower petals float down and bees buzz past. I remember how Dad used to say it was the closest thing to snow the valley would ever see. I reach out and catch one of those snowflake petals in my hand.

"Kate, what happened to your hair?"

I don't remind Grammy that I'd talked to her about it before on the phone. Telling someone they've already heard something doesn't help them remember any better.

"I got gum in my hair when I was trying to spy on Sofia with her new friend, Marisa."

"Spying? Good heavens, child, this isn't the Cold War. Why were you spying?"

I sigh and tell her everything about Sofia and Marisa. I don't know if it's harder or easier to tell things to someone who is going to forget everything you say. On one hand, I never have to worry about Grammy telling anyone else. On the other hand, it's sort of like when we ran out of clean washcloths and I tried pouring water over one of mom's special dusting rags. It just rolled off in big old beads.

"Sounds like you need some magic," says Grammy.

"Yeah, that's what you said on Friday."

Grammy chuckles. "Well, a broken clock is right twice a day. And I'm right about this."

"Like rabbits out of a hat?"

"Oh, no," says Grammy. "That's not real magic. That's tricks and sleight of hand. I'm talking about Everyday Magic."

I shake my head. "I don't believe in magic."

"That's too bad," says Grammy. "It only works if you believe in it. That's the first rule of Everyday Magic."

We get to the house, with the gravel driveway covered in weeds, waiting for Dad to come home and pull them. Grammy opens the front door.

I don't think I believe her. This is all probably just a part of Grammy getting older and her brain not working how it used to. But her eyes sparkle the way they do when she's really in her mind and seeing me, so I keep her talking. It's nice to have her actually be here. "How does it work? How would it help with Sofia?"

She taps her chin. "Well, when I was younger, my best

friend, Alice, was mad at me for kissing . . . oh, what was his name? It doesn't matter. I made her a magical gum-wrapper necklace and said sorry. We went right back to being friends again. Just like it never even happened."

"That doesn't sound like magic. That sounds like making up."

"Hmmmm." Grammy sets her gold bag on the floor. "That is one way to look at it. But I think forgiving someone is a special kind of magic."

I can't help wondering, though. If Grammy believes in magic and if forgiveness is a special kind of magic, why hasn't she used it on Dad yet? I cross my arms. "I still don't believe it."

"Well, if you don't believe it, you'll never see it."

# Chapter 12

*G*rammy walks to Dad's office and opens the door. "I think I'm going to lie down," she says. "All the excitement wore me out. Thanks, Kate."

As soon as the latch clicks, I go into the kitchen and pour myself a bowl of cereal. I can't help thinking of what Sofia said to Marisa. *Something Kate and I used to do . . . Kind of silly.*

I know what Sensei would say about those thoughts. The same thing he said to me on Friday when I was so tired from the jumping side kick. *Do not focus on the pain. Focus only on the next move.* But I still don't know what my next move should be when Mom walks in the door. I step out of the kitchen to greet her. She throws her keys in her purse, kicks off her heels and says, "Where's Pat?"

"She's in bed."

"Oh, good." Mom shakes her hair out and pulls it into a ponytail. "Sounds like I need to find someone to come in and watch her immediately."

"Watch her? Like a babysitter?"

Mom nods and takes out her earrings.

"Grammy's not a little kid." In my mind, I hear Miss Williams calling her *dear* again.

"No, but she needs help. What if she didn't walk into your school but went somewhere else, and we didn't know where she was?"

"She would've remembered eventually," I argue. "She doesn't want to be treated like a baby."

Mom pulls me into a hug and strokes my head like I'm a lost kitten. I stay stiff against her arms. "Oh, Katydid, this is all part of the . . . What is in your hair?"

"Gum. Remember?"

"Oh, yes." Mom nudges me back into the kitchen. "What are you doing with chewing gum? Isn't it against school rules?"

"It wasn't me. I was on the ground and sort of fell under a desk—"

"Why were you on the ground?"

I sigh and mumble, "I was . . . spying."

Mom raises an eyebrow. "On who?"

"Sofia and Marisa."

"Who's Marisa?"

"Sofia's new friend. They had a sleepover together on Friday."

Mom walks to the cupboard and opens it. "Why were you spying on them?"

"Because . . . well, I said something mean about Marisa

and I knew she was mad at me and I thought maybe she was saying mean things about me to Sofia."

Mom sighs. She stands on her tiptoes to reach for the jar of peanut butter on the second highest shelf.

The peanut butter used to be on the highest shelf. Every time we needed it, she'd call Dad in to help her get it down. He used to walk into the kitchen, flexing his muscles.

*"Stand aside; let your man help his damsel in distress."*

*She rolled her eyes and pushed him away. "I don't need any help. I'm an independent woman!"*

We don't put anything on the top shelf anymore.

"Katydid, do you remember when I ran Mayor Gerton's very first campaign?"

I shrug. I know where this is going. Another one of Mom's public relations lessons. Everything in life is about public relations.

She sets the peanut butter on the counter and puts her hand on my shoulder. "The last mayor, the guy we were running against, ran a really nasty campaign. Lots of attack ads all over the place. But do you know what we did?"

I shake my head.

"We spoke only in positive terms. Didn't run a single negative ad. And people responded. Obviously. We won in a landslide." She takes her hand off my shoulder and points at me; that's how I know she's about to tell me the lesson I'm supposed to learn from all of this. "You catch more flies with honey. Not vinegar. Mean and nasty attacks are not the way to make sure Sofia's still your friend." Her voice softens. "You're better than that."

"I know. I'm sorry." I really am. Mostly because of the gum in my hair. But also a little bit because I can't help thinking about Sensei, and how kindness is strength—and today I wasn't kind or strong.

Mom wraps her finger around a piece of my hair above my shoulders. "Friends are a tough thing," she says. "I remember those days." I can tell she's about to launch into another of her therapy talks where we hash out our feelings and discuss everything over and over, around and around. It makes me tired just thinking about it.

"Mom. I don't . . ." I shrug. "I don't want to talk about it anymore." Her mouth hangs open for a second before she shakes her head and unscrews the lid. She takes out a great big sloppy goop of peanut butter, and spreads it right over the bubblegum. She goes on picking and slicking for a minute before wiping off her hands and asking, "So how was the rest of school?"

"I wrote a poem." I pull the folded-up paper out of my pocket.

Mom twists her finger around the gray patch of hair near her ears as she reads it. Finally, she sniffs and says, "That is really lovely. Truly, Katydid." She reads it again and then points at the part Jane circled. "Why are these lines marked?"

"That was Jane's favorite part."

Mom sets my poem on the counter and rests her elbows on either side of it, leaning way over. "Mine, too."

"That's the problem," I grumble. "Now I'm supposed to use the part of me mentioned in those lines to do a presentation."

"What's wrong with that?"

"Everyone . . . Sofia . . . they want me to sing."

Mom's mouth forms a silent O.

I take the paper back and smooth it out again, thinking that if it was a year ago, this wouldn't be a problem. A year ago, I could still pick up that guitar in my room and run my thumb across the strings. A year ago, that was the easiest way to get Dad's attention.

*"You playing?" He asked, poking his head inside my bedroom. I nodded. "I'm tinkering."*

*"May I join you?"*

*"Mmmhmmm." My tongue stuck out between my teeth as I tried to lay my pointer finger flat across all the strings. I strummed a chord, but it came out buzzy and off pitch, and I growled. "I can't get this bar chord!"*

*"Ah, yes. When you can do that, you'll know you're a real guitar player."*

*Dad took his guitar and played the chord like it was the easiest thing in the world. "You just need to grow a little more."*

*"I don't have time for that."*

*"Sure, you do. But don't grow up just yet, okay?" And then his fingers started plucking a familiar set of four notes—ba-da-da-dum, ba-da-da-dum—like a rolling wave, and I knew our favorite song was coming. He sang in a voice that was almost a whisper. "So shut your eyes while daddy sings of wonderful sights that be. And you shall see the beautiful things as you rock in the misty sea."*

My fingers tap the rhythm of that song. "Part of me . . . wants to sing."

Mom says too fast, "I wish you would."

But then I remember the almost crying on Friday after karate when I played that E-minor chord on Dad's guitar. The way all my sadness stayed squarely where it was, not even budging a little bit, and my eyes burned hot and blurry.

I shake my head. Mom wouldn't understand. She likes to cry. She watches sad movies some nights and before she starts them says, "I just need a good cry."

A few minutes later, Mom's just barely finished rinsing all the peanut butter and gum out of my hair when there's a knock at the door.

"Who could that be?" Mom dries her hands and heads out of the kitchen. I'm getting off the counter when I hear her say, "Oh, Parker. Come in."

I try to check my reflection in the microwave. It's too dark. My hair is wet, so I probably look bad. But I don't care, because Parker is in my house. I take a deep breath and walk into the entrance hall. "Hey, Parker."

He's holding a notebook and two textbooks stacked on top of each other. "Hi, Kate. I brought your assignments for what you missed after you left."

"Well, that was thoughtful," says Mom.

I rush over and take the books out of his arms. "Thanks."

Mom puts her hand on Parker's shoulder and looks out the front door. "Did your Mom bring you over here, honey?"

"Yep."

"Hmmmm." Mom takes a step toward the door. "I think I have an idea. I need to talk to her, though. Do you mind hanging out here with Kate for a little bit?"

Parker shrugs. "That's cool."

Mom goes outside, leaving me and Parker staring at the walls, the floor, the ceiling. Anything but each other. I set the books on the hall table, but don't put them far enough back, and they fall off, slamming to the floor. Parker and I both hurry to pick them up. But the first thing I spot is a bookmark that says, *Books Are Magic*.

I pick it up and think about Grammy and her Everyday Magic.

"Oh, that's mine," says Parker, as he puts the books on the

table. "I used it to mark our spot in the science book. You can keep it."

"Thanks." I place the bookmark on the stack of books.

"You got the gum out," Parker says, pointing at my wet hair.

"Oh. Yeah. Peanut butter."

Parker nods. It's quiet. He's still holding *The Hobbit*, and he brings it in front of him, ready to start reading at any moment.

"Do you want a snack?" I say. "There's pretzels in the cabinet. Remember how we always used to make silly faces with pretzels?"

"Yeah, I remember." Parker chuckles. "That was fun. But my Mom has this new rule about only having fruits and vegetables for after-school snacks."

"Okay." I look in the kitchen for something, anything to help me hang out with Parker and not seem so boring that he has to go back to reading his book. "How about an orange?" Oranges are kind of exciting and interesting, right?

"Awesome."

We both sit down at the kitchen table, and I peel an orange.

"So have you heard from your dad lately?" Parker asks.

The question is a kick straight to my chest. I've never talked to Parker about my dad, but he probably heard from his Mom. "No." I hand him the peeled orange and try to act like it doesn't matter.

Parker coughs. "Not at all?"

"I'm sure we will soon." I grab another orange and dig my fingernail into the skin. "He'll come back. His guitar is still here." I rip orange slices away from each other so hard that juice squirts out. "So . . . what did you think of school today?"

"It was different than I imagined. But good."

"Did you even pay attention to any of it?" I point at *The Hobbit* sitting next to him on the table.

Parker gives a sheepish smile. "It's hard to put down a good book. I've never had to before because my mom let me read as long as I wanted."

"Well, maybe try to put it down tomorrow." I laugh. "Or you'll be the smartest person I know who fails fifth grade."

"Okay, fine." Parker pops an orange slice into his mouth. "Thanks, Kate."

My cheeks feel hot and I turn away.

Mom and Mrs. Harris walk in then. Mom is holding Parker's little sister, Amelie, a chunky baby wrapped in a pink blanket. "I'm sorry she's such a poor sleeper."

Mrs. Harris grimaces. "She'll grow out of it someday. I hope." She sits down at the table while Mom bounces Amelie up and down. Amelie starts crying, a high, strangled-sounding scream.

"Oh. I'll let you deal with that." Mom hands the baby back to Mrs. Harris. "It's been eleven years since I've had one of those. I won't lie. I've forgotten what to do."

I turn back to Parker. "So do you think we'll learn a new move at karate this Friday?"

Parker's got his book open, but he's looking at his mom with Amelie, who's still screaming and screaming.

Although Mom tries to keep talking with Mrs. Harris, it's no use. "You know what? I'll call you later."

"Please!" Mrs. Harris laughs and rolls her eyes. "I swear, every day from three to seven it's the same thing."

"The witching hour," Mom says.

"I don't remember Parker being quite so . . . consistent."

Mrs. Harris bounces Amelie back to the front door, and Parker stands up. "Well, see ya," he says.

"See ya."

Mom shuts the door as they pull out of the driveway. "That was productive."

"It was?"

"Mrs. Harris is going to watch Grammy for the next few days until I can find something more permanent. Maybe a daycare."

"A daycare? And what about Amelie?"

"It's only a few days," says Mom. "I need her to stay here and make sure Pat doesn't leave. She said she can hold a crying baby here just as well as she can at home. I'll look for a daycare in the meantime."

I'm about to argue more about daycare for Grammy, but Mom stops me before I even begin. "We knew this was coming, Katydid. Let me be the grown-up. I'm just trying to take care of everyone, okay?"

♪ ♪ ♪

That night after dinner, Grammy is sitting on the couch with her knitting. I sit next to her, finishing up my math homework. Mom closes her computer, takes a deep breath, and looks at me.

"Katydid, do you want to play some music with me?"

I don't even look up from the problem I'm doing. "It's just Kate. And no."

"I really wish you would. It's been so long. Ever since . . ." her voice trails off and she doesn't finish the sentence, but I do.

"Ever since Dad left."

The truth thuds to the ground, a cement brick, echoing.

But Grammy doesn't seem to notice. "My Tony always made the best music. Voice of an angel. You know for my birthday one year, he wrote me a song. What I wouldn't give to hear him sing again."

And even though what Grammy's saying is true, it feels like lies. Hundreds of pretendings all adding up into a great big nothing. An empty space.

"If you sing with me now, you might feel comfortable doing it for your presentation at school," says Mom, "Maybe it will help if we sing together. Like we used to."

I drop my pencil, letting it roll into the space between the couch cushions. "Like we used to? Dad's not here. I can't sing without him. All it sounds like is . . . a big black hole. It hurts."

Mom blinks and whispers, "Excuse me." She walks super fast to the music room, closes the door, and begins playing the piano. That's what Mom does when she needs to cry about Dad. She plays that rumbling piece by Beethoven, *Pathétique*. It makes my insides feel all shaky. Sometimes I wonder if that's why she plays it. So that by the end she doesn't know if she's feeling that way because of the missing or the music.

I finish the last few math problems, pushing too hard on the end of the pencil when the piano gets louder and louder. Grammy keeps trying to make something with her knitting needles, but only ends up with more and more yarn snarls.

I get up to put my homework in my backpack but accidentally knock over Grammy's gold bag. The letter from earlier slides out and onto the floor.

Mom's music changes from light ups and downs back to the last slow, shaking bass notes. As I pick up the envelope, I notice the empty space under Dad's name again. The whiteness that should be filled up with an address, a connection, a knowing. Then I think about the box of notes under my bed, each one waiting for the same thing. I have no idea how I'm going to keep my promise to Grammy to get her letter to Dad. But if I don't try, we're all going to be stuck here, empty and waiting between the notes of *Pathétique*.

I open the door to the music room. "Mom?"

"Yes, Katydid?" She's done playing and is in the black recliner with a book on her lap. Her eyes are pink.

"I was wondering if you had Dad's address. I want to send him a letter. Well, really, it's Grammy's letter, but I promised—"

"You know the answer to that, honey." Mom looks back down at her book. "I don't know where he is." She turns pages way too fast to actually be reading.

I nod. "Right. I know. Just making sure."

After closing the door, I go to my room and add Grammy's letter to all of my own.

*Dear Dad,*

*I've decided I hate promises. After all, you promised Mom you'd stay with her through happiness and sorrow. But when sorrow poured in like a mudslide, you just ran away. From Mom, from me, from everything. I don't ever want to hear the words "I promise" again.*

*Love,*
*Kate*

# Chapter 13

*A*ll night, I dream that I'm trying to sing but no
sound comes out. It gets caught in my throat, blocked by
something invisible and heavy. Guitar strings break under my
fingers with a sharp twang. Then Dad walks in. He picks up
his guitar and sits next to me, smiling, not saying anything.
The heaviness disappears. He starts plucking arpeggios and
singing . . . something.

I wake up humming. For a moment I feel all filled up
having the music back. Then I remember that it was just a
dream and Dad's still gone.

I can't fall back asleep, so I go to the window to see the
fog settling in the orchard.

Suddenly, Grammy walks into my room and turns on the
light. "Oh, good. You're up."

My clock says 5:30, so I sit down next to my pile of blankets. "No, I'm going back to bed. I just wanted to . . ." I point out the window.

Grammy doesn't look. She's balancing her knitting needles and a big ball of yarn. With a huff, she plops down on my bed and puts her knitting to the side. "I'm losing it, aren't I?"

"Losing what?"

"Oh, you know. Everything. These pieces of me that used to be organized up here just fine." She points at her head. "They keep shuffling around. Sometimes I can't find them at all."

"Oh. Yeah. A little." I've never heard Grammy talk about her sickness before. I tap my fingers on the mattress.

"I'm not going to be here much longer. At least, this part of me. The real me."

Usually when people say bad things about themselves, you're supposed to tell them they're wrong. But what Grammy is saying is true, and it doesn't seem like denying it is what she really wants anyway. But maybe I can put it in a way that doesn't sound quite so bad.

"The doctor said it will happen slowly. Come and go. She said it will take time for you to . . . lose everything."

"When you're my age, dear, time is a slippery thing. There's never enough left." Grammy sighs and picks her knitting back up. "Well, I'm here now, I guess." She makes three stitches, shakes her head, and takes one out. "Oh, rats!" She puts the knitting in her lap. "Can you help me with something?"

"Yeah, sure."

Grammy lifts a needle with an orange rectangle hanging from it. "Will you help me finish this? I've been trying to make you something. A little bit of magic to help you sing again. Even if your dad's not here."

"More magic?"

"Not just any magic. This is proven Everyday Magic. I've seen it work."

"When?"

"When your father was a little boy. Just a bit younger than you."

"Really?" There's a part of me that wants to believe in magic, especially if it has anything to do with Dad.

"Oh, yes," says Grammy. "When my Tony was a little boy he was scared of everything. Everything! Snails, flies, trains, germs, sandals, chalk, thunderstorms. Everything. So one night I made him a beautiful blue hat, and the next morning I gave it to him and said I'd filled it up with all my love and courage and it would protect him and keep him brave. And you know what?"

"What?" I scoot closer to her.

"It worked."

"No way."

Grammy nods and puts her needle through a loop of yarn. "He came home from school that day and said he hadn't been scared once but was sure he'd used up all the magic. So that night I knitted a red hat for him. And the next night a yellow one. I made him a hat in every color imaginable."

"For how long?"

"One year, two months, and eighteen days."

"That's a long time." I wrap my finger around the string of orange yarn.

Grammy nods in rhythm to the knitting needles. "Then one day he told me he didn't need a hat anymore. I was done."

"I bet that was nice."

"I was happy to have my evenings back, and my fingers

sure needed the break." She laughs and cracks a knuckle. "But I was a little sad, too. It's nice to be needed."

We sit there thinking about that for a second. About being needed. Until Grammy says, "But now my brain seems to be working against me. I keep forgetting the pattern of stitches. No matter how many times I say it to myself, it slips away. So I need your help. Will you?"

I look at the clock, and the sky outside, not even orange yet. I really want to go back to sleep. But I want the magic more. The magic I can't quite believe in, but want to.

"I don't know how to knit."

"Oh, it's not hard," says Grammy. "I'll teach you, and you can do these last couple rows in a jiffy."

She hands me the knitting needles as if she's giving me a fragile little bird. "Now careful with these. They're very old. I knitted all my Tony's baby booties on those needles. Countless winter scarves for when we visited the mountains. And all those hats." She stares off somewhere, probably thinking of Dad.

They're old-fashioned and wooden, with small red balls on the ends of them. I hold the knitting needles as gently as if they were almond blossoms, running my fingers over the slightly pocked and dented wood surfaces. "You still have these? They never broke?"

"Things last a long time when you take good care of them." Grammy leans over. "Now listen carefully. In through the front door, around the back. Peep through the window, off jumps Jack!"

We get to work learning to knit after that. The rhyme makes it sound easy. It's not. Knitting needles are like chopsticks, and yarn is slippery like noodles, but instead of just getting noodles to my mouth I'm trying to twist them around each other and make knots.

Grammy hands me a piece of paper that says *K2, skip 1. Repeat to end.*

"Here's the dang pattern I keep forgetting." She shows me how to do it once and then hands the needles back.

It takes me a couple tries to remember, too. But eventually, knitting starts to take on a rhythm, like doing the kata in karate. Each move flows smoothly into the next, leaving my brain a place to just be.

I don't have very much more to do before the magic hat is finished. The karate feeling is gone all too soon.

Grammy teaches me how to cinch the top and stitch up the side. All of a sudden, that rectangle is a real live orange hat.

"See?" she says. "It's like magic."

I rub the bumpy edge between my thumb and pointer finger. "Almost."

"Almost," says Grammy. "You sure are hard to please. Now just wear that the next time you need to sing, and see if it doesn't help."

"Like for my presentation?"

"Or when your mom asks."

A frown pulls at my mouth when I think about last night. How angry I was. "I don't know."

"You've got to believe in the magic."

I stretch the brim across my fingers.

"Your dad did," Grammy whispers.

I pull the hat over my tangled hair. "How do I look?"

Grammy's eyes get all crinkly. "Like a memory."

Mom walks in then. "Oh, Katydid. You're up. And Pat. What are you two girls doing?"

Grammy makes her way to the door and pats Mom on the shoulder. "Just making some magic." She winks at me and leaves the room.

"Nice hat," says Mom.

"Thanks."

She leans against the door frame. "I'm sorry about last night," she says. "I shouldn't have pushed you. I just miss singing with . . . you."

"It's okay. I'm sorry, too."

"So what do you think you'll do for your presentation if you aren't going to sing?"

"I don't know." I tuck an itchy piece of hair underneath the hat and remember how Grammy said it made Dad brave. "Maybe I could still sing. I'm thinking about it."

"Really?" Mom whispers, straightening up.

I tug at the edges of my hat and nod.

"Oh, Katydid," Mom leaves the doorway, crosses the room in three strides, and hugs me. "I would love that so much. It would feel—"

"I haven't decided for sure yet."

"Yes, I know." She nods and backs away. Just before she leaves the room, she says, "I'll be interested to hear your decision."

As I walk out the door that morning, Grammy grabs my shoulder and hands me the knitted hat. I'd left it at the breakfast table. "Remember, Kate," she whispers. "Remember my Tony. Believe."

And I want to. I really do.

# Part II
## Give

# Chapter 14

"**S**o you didn't have to cut all your hair off," Jane says as we walk into school. Everyone's bodies are pushing past us, and my elbow gets knocked by someone when I reach up to touch the place in my sandy-blond hair that used to be sticky.

"Yeah. My mom says peanut butter always works."

Jane gives a single, short nod. "Good. Even though . . ." She squints at me and cocks her head. "You would make a very handsome boy."

"Hey!"

"Want me to draw you as one?"

"No way!" I laugh as we reach our lockers and open them.

Jane pulls out her big black sketchbook, and we walk into class. "Okay. Kate the pretty, pretty princess it is."

"Don't you dare," I say loud enough to draw Sofia's attention. She watches me take my seat and nods hello.

I nod back.

It's such a cold, weird way to greet my best friend. I mean, Mom nods hello at strangers while she drives.

♪ ♪ ♪

All morning, I reach into my sweater pocket to touch the magic hat waiting there. I want to believe Grammy, to believe that it will make that empty, aching silence in my heart go away and bring back the music, but it's hard to imagine anything can do that, especially a simple hat.

When Miss Reynolds starts going over the list of people we can choose for our poems, I can't help but take it out to see if I feel anything when I hold it. Maybe just a spark of magic.

"What's that?" whispers Parker.

I almost jump out of my chair. Parker is getting close to the end of *The Hobbit*. The way he's been flipping his pages almost fast enough to rip them out means it's getting good. He usually never talks when he's at a good part in a book.

"Oh, it's just a hat I knitted. Or helped knit. It's nothing, really." The girl in front of me, Amy, peeks over her shoulder. I look away from Parker and stuff the hat back in my pocket.

"That's pretty cool," Parker whispers. "I wish I could do that."

"Maybe I can . . . teach you." The words almost stick in my throat. I wait for them to burst into flames or something horrible.

"Awesome," says Parker.

All of a sudden, I think I can ace any presentation.

Before we move to work with our partners, I reach into my pocket, pull the hat back out, and stuff it so hard over my head that a few strands of hair pull out.

"Okay, class. Find your partner, grab a laptop, and get to work!"

Jane comes to me this time. She's holding a silver laptop

and sits in the desk Parker just left. "Nice hat!"

I touch it. "Oh, thanks."

Jane opens the laptop, turns it on, and passes it to me. "So I was thinking we should do our presentation on George Washington. Because I like to draw cherry trees."

"Isn't that a myth?"

Jane rolls her eyes. "Does it matter?"

"Probably." I laugh.

"Okay, fine. Lots of blood and guts then. I'm good at that, too."

"Eeewww."

"Hey!" Jane points at me. "You wanted me to stick with the facts. The Revolutionary War wasn't something from a Monet painting."

"Okay, fine."

Jane pulls out her black sketchbook and opens it, slowly, like each page is soaking into her thoughts. Finally, she says, "If you let me draw cherry trees . . . I won't make you sing."

"What?"

Jane shrugs. "I watched you when Miss Reynolds suggested it. And then when Sofia freaked out about it. I could see that you maybe didn't want to."

Out of the corner of my eye, I see Sofia and Marisa pretending to dance in their seats, obviously planning to perform. If I sang too, maybe Sofia would think I was good enough for sleepovers and phone calls again. That hat on my head suddenly feels scratchy and a little tight. Is that what magic feels like? "Well, actually, I think . . . maybe I could try to sing."

"Really?" Jane looks up from her sketchbook. "Are you sure?"

"Yeah, I mean . . . I haven't done it in a while. But—" I touch the hat.

"Well, try now," Jane says with a small clap. "Just really

quiet so only I can hear. Ooohhh, we are going to have the best presentation. Maybe I can draw a whole mural. And you . . . you could put on a mini-musical about his life."

"What about the poem we have to write for him?"

Jane waves her hands. "Details. We'll work that in somewhere."

Jane goes on and on. Her eyes get wider and wider and her ideas grow bigger and bigger, until I think she might decide to sell tickets if I don't stop her soon.

"Maybe we should just write the poem first."

Jane stops mid-sentence, her mouth hanging open, then says, "Good idea. After you sing for me."

I pull the hat down over my ears.

"I promise to give you a standing ovation," Jane whispers.

"Please don't."

"Okay. Sorry." Jane mimes flipping a switch. "Rainbow Lab turned off."

I take a deep breath, close my eyes, and wait for the magic.

I try to remember the words to a song. Any song. Instead, all I can think about is Mom sitting at the piano, opening up her music book with the cover falling off from being used so many times.

*"What do you feel like singing tonight, Katydid?"*

*I twisted the knobs on the neck of my guitar, tuning my D string to get it just right. "I don't know. What do you think, Dad?"*

*He was sitting on the couch. His eyes flicked up from his phone. "You have such a pretty voice, Katydid. Why don't you do all the singing tonight?"*

*My guitar felt a tiny bit heavier.*

*Mom turned around on the piano bench. "Tony, are you sure?"*

*He shrugged. Didn't even look up from his phone.*

I pull the hat down tighter over my head and pinch my eyes closed even harder. "Come on. Come on. Come on," I whisper.

*"Come on, Elizabeth," Dad said, pulling his guitar strap over his head and walking into the kitchen. "I've got to play some music today. I'll go crazy if I don't."*

*Mom held out a letter. "We just got this. You told me you took care of it."*

*Dad grabbed the letter and read it. "Oh, I . . . I forgot."*

*"I asked you to do that at least five times."*

*"I've been tired, okay?"*

*"And I'm not tired?" Mom snapped.*

*"Look, I'll take care of it this time. I promise. Just come play the piano."*

*"I can't," said Mom. "I have to deal with this because I can't trust you to do it."*

*"I'll play with you, Dad." I hopped down from the kitchen counter.*

*"No," he said. "I don't feel like singing anymore."*

A hot weight sinks to the bottom of my stomach. The space behind my eyes burns. A knot forms in my throat. If I open my mouth now, all that'll come out is a sob. It's right then that I realize Grammy is a liar. A big, fat, muumuu-wearing, hat-knitting liar. There isn't a drop of magic in this hat. Not one.

I open my eyes and shake my head.

Jane reaches out her hand like she's about to touch me and then pulls back. "It's okay," she says. "You don't have to."

We get to work researching George Washington's childhood. The cherry tree thing really is a myth, but Jane says she's still drawing and writing about it since everyone believes it anyway, and "Art isn't just about things that actually happened." She says this as she scribbles the words, *I'm from a myth.*

It turns out George Washington's dad died when he was eleven. I wonder if maybe George Washington would have been something softer than a soldier if his dad had been around.

"We should talk about that in our poem," I whisper to Jane. "About his dad dying."

Jane nods and holds the pen above the paper we're writing our first draft on. "How do you see or touch death . . . without being gross?" Jane asks. "Poetry shouldn't be gross."

I think about how things felt and sounded after Dad left. "Maybe talk about the sound of his mom crying."

"Oh, that's good! And there had to be a grave. Let's mention that, too."

Right before the lunch bell rings, Jane gives me her cell phone number so we can talk about our presentation after school. I give her my mom's number.

"You don't have your own phone?" Jane asks.

"No," I say, embarrassed. "My mom says I can't have one until I turn fourteen."

"Bummer." Jane folds the paper with my mom's phone number on it and puts it in her pocket. "I really do like that hat. It's cool."

I forgot I had it on. I take off the magic-less hat and look at the stupid orange stitches. Orange is the only color Jane isn't wearing today, so I slide the hat across the desk to her. "You can have it, if you want."

"Really?" She puts it on right away. "How do I look?"

"Colorful."

Jane grins. "Perfect!"

# Chapter 15

**W**hen I enter the cafeteria, I walk over to the table where Sofia is sitting with Marisa. Sofia doesn't have any pink on today, and after the way she spoke yesterday about my singing, I can't help thinking that maybe she isn't mad at me anymore.

At the table, Marisa and Sofia lean into each other, and the air is abuzz with Spanish words. Their mouths move quickly, so quickly that I can't catch on to a single word to figure out what they're saying.

I clear my throat to cut through their bubbling voices. "Hi, Sofia."

Both she and Marisa stop talking immediately and look at me like I walked in on a private moment. "Hi, Kate." Sofia smiles, but I can tell she's nervous because she reaches for her necklace.

"I'm . . . sorry about yesterday." I wish Marisa wasn't hearing this. But Sensei once said that the first person to apologize is the strongest person, and I want to make up for not being strong yesterday.

"Me too," says Sofia. She pats the seat to her left. "Want to sit down?"

"Okay." I pull the chair out slowly, trying not to let it screech along the floor and topple this peace between Sofia and me that feels like a wobbly tower of blocks. When I sit down, I pull my sandwich out of my paper bag.

"So," says Marisa. She leans forward, and her long brown braid swishes onto the table. It has a pink ribbon tied to the end. "Sofia said your grandma just moved in with you because she can't remember stuff anymore."

I freeze with my turkey sandwich halfway to my mouth.

"Is that true? Is she like that movie my mom watches all the time . . . *The Notebook*? Do you have to read her life story to her every day?"

I cram my sandwich back into my lunch bag and stand up. "You told her?" I growl.

Sofia looks at Marisa and then at me. "I didn't know it was a secret."

"Of course it was a secret!"

"I'm sorry."

I don't even care that Sofia's the stronger person this time for apologizing first, because she should apologize. But I can't say it's okay because that would be a lie, and Sensei says honesty is the only way to have any other virtue. So I march away from that table, away from Sofia, away from stupid pink ribbons, and across the cafeteria to where Jane's sitting with Brooklyn and Emma.

I throw my lunch sack onto the table and fall into a chair.

"Well, hi," says Jane. She's holding a fork in one hand and a blue pastel in the other. Her sketchbook is open in front of her and there's a Tupperware container to the side of it. "Nice to see you here."

I don't say anything.

Brooklyn and Emma stop chewing their sandwiches and look at me. They're cousins and both pretty quiet, although I sat next to Brooklyn in class last year, and she can be really funny.

"Hi, Kate," she says.

"Hi, Brooklyn."

Jane puts down the pastel and waves her fork. "Anyone want some eggplant stir-fry? My grandma made it. It tastes better than it sounds, I promise."

Brooklyn shakes her head, but Emma takes her own fork and tries some.

"Yeah, sure. Thanks." I say.

Jane hands me an extra plastic fork and pushes the container towards me. The stir-fry is a little cold, and the eggplant pieces look different than the eggplant my mom grows, but it still tastes better than anything I've ever had at the Chinese restaurants in town. "This is better than Wonderful House."

Jane laughs. "Of course it is. It's *real* Chinese food. There's a difference." Then Jane alternates between eating, drawing, and making little jokes to Brooklyn and Emma, who are working on some kind of braided bracelets. I feel a bit left out with no project of my own, so I try to figure out what Jane's sketching. But it's not very clear right now, and if I ask, it might hurt her feelings. Artists think you should know what you're looking at without asking.

After a few minutes, Jane sighs, smudges a few marks, and throws down her pastel. She leans back in her chair and pulls on the edge of that orange hat as she looks at me. "So I was thinking about your poem and . . ." She pauses. "I like the part about karate just as much as the part about music."

"So I don't have to sing," I whisper.

Jane shrugs, "If you want. Or we could play a song on my phone or something for music instead. If you still wanted to focus on—"

"No!" I blurt out. "Karate's good." My shoulders relax and I take a deep breath. "I love karate."

Jane stares at the ceiling for a minute, thinking, and then grins. "George Washington, karate master."

Brooklyn and Emma giggle.

"It sounds silly when you say it like that." I poke at the stir-fry and my mouth twitches upward.

Jane's smile gets wider. "Maybe he didn't need an axe to chop down that cherry tree."

"Well, it could explain why he was so sneaky crossing the Delaware."

That gets Jane going. For the rest of lunch, we keep trading ninja George Washington jokes. Brooklyn and Emma, who apparently watch lots of action movies together, start planning a script for a show with George Washington played by Jackie Chan. And I forget about the deep crack widening between me and Sofia.

As we're walking back to class, Sofia and Marisa cut in front of us. I stop in my tracks, watching them enter the room.

Jane tilts her head to the side. "You guys used to be best friends, didn't you?"

"We're still best friends," I say. "Things have just been . . .

hard lately. We'll work it out. She'll come back around."

Jane pulls a folded slip of paper out of her pocket, reads it, and then puts it back. "I don't know. People who love you don't need to come back around. They never leave to begin with."

But I know that can't be right, because what would that mean about Dad?

♪ ♪ ♪

After school, when I cross the street to get to the road leading to my house, Parker runs up and joins me. "My mom's at your place today," he says. "Can I walk with you?"

"Sure." I glance behind me, wondering if anyone from school sees us, but I don't think anyone does. As we walk, his elbow keeps bumping into mine, and every time it does I have to press my lips together to keep from smiling.

"I saw Jane wearing your hat," he says. "She really likes it."

"I didn't want it anymore."

"My mom would be so mad if I gave away something she knitted. It takes a long time."

"Your mom knits?"

Parker kicks at a pebble. "She used to. The baby doesn't let her do much of anything these days."

"Oh. Yeah. Does she cry like that all the time?"

"It feels like it some days."

"Sorry."

Parker shrugs. He opens his new book and reads while he walks. I can't think of anything interesting enough to distract him from reading, so I don't say anything.

We're both silent as we pass the orchard. Only the bees

are buzzing. Speaking must be harder when you're human.

Before we even get to my house, we can hear Amelie screaming. Parker's mom bursts out the front door the moment we start up the porch steps. "Come on, buddy! I have to get Amelie home."

Parker and his mom both wave goodbye before getting in their van and driving away.

When I walk inside, Grammy calls from the living room, "Kate, how'd everything go today?"

That's when I remember I'm still mad about the magic. Or the not-magic, really.

"Awful. The hat didn't work. There was no magic."

Grammy pats the seat on the couch right next to her. "I was afraid that might happen."

"So you lied to me?" I throw myself into the couch hard. I want Grammy to know just how mad I am. But the leather gobbles up my anger, sucking me deep down in the cushions.

"Lie? Pish-posh. I didn't lie. The magic is real. But you know me and my brain. I forgot the second rule of Everyday Magic."

"Another rule?"

"Of course. What? You thought there was only one rule?"

I fold my arms and wait. I won't be tricked this time.

"This morning when I had you help me finish the hat, I broke the second rule. You have to *give* the magic to someone. And since you helped finish the hat, well, you couldn't keep it for yourself and have Everyday Magic."

"Why not?" I ask. "What's the point of magic if you can't make it for yourself?"

Grammy clamps her hands on her legs and stands up. "Oh, don't you think that when you give magic to someone else, a little bit of it will come back around to you?"

"I don't know. I haven't seen the magic yet."

Grammy walks into the kitchen. "Good point. So where is this disappointing hat?"

"I gave it to Jane."

I hear cupboards bang open and closed and metal bowls clanging around. "Who's Jane?" Grammy asks.

"She's a . . . friend." I go to the kitchen and sit on a stool. "A new friend. Sofia and I got in a fight, so I sat with Jane at lunch today. It was fun, actually."

Grammy straightens up. She's holding a wooden spoon. "So you're saying you gave the hat you helped make to this Jane girl, and then found comfort in your hour of need?"

I shrug. "Yeah, I guess."

"Hmmm," she says with a wink. "Sounds like magic to me."

# Chapter 16

*I* still think Grammy is lying about the Everyday Magic. "I don't know," I say. "It sort of feels like you're making this up."

Grammy points the spoon at her head and says, "Katherine, I can barely keep track of my truths, let alone make up some lies to remember as well. Now you might not believe me, but I'm going to prove it to you. We're going to make some magic for your mother."

"Mom? Why?"

"Why not?" Grammy puts an apron over her head. "You don't want her asking about that . . . your . . . uh . . ." she hums. "You know." She hums some more.

"My singing?"

"That's the ticket. See what I mean with this . . ." She fumbles tying the knot behind her apron and when she looks at me again I can see part of her is slipping away.

I try to pull her back. "What's the magic?"

She blinks. "Magic. Magic. Oh, yes. I was going to make the cookies. My special cookies. I . . ." She sits on the stool next to me and fights to bring back the part of herself that's walking away down some dark path. "I can't remember. What are my special cookies?"

"I don't know."

"Yes, you do. Yes, you do. How could you forget?" She scrunches her fists up by her eyes. "They were my Tony's favorites. He had them every day after school and even when he was grown up I'd make them. It was a secret. My secret cookies. Kate, what are my secret cookies?"

That's when I know what she's talking about.

"Peanut butter," I say. "Your secret-recipe peanut-butter cookies."

"Oh, yes," says Grammy. "Thank you." She pats my knee and stands back up, shuffling over to the other side of the counter. She pulls out a few ingredients: peanut butter, sugar, a knife, some measuring spoons. Then stops. "I don't remember how to make them. Peanut butter, sugar, eggs. But how much? How could I forget this?"

"Don't you have a recipe somewhere?"

Grammy stares down the hallway. More of her is drifting away. Suddenly she whispers, "Yes. A recipe." Those words seem to reel in the rest of herself. "A recipe! A recipe. Yes, Katherine. I have the recipe. It's in that box. The picture box I'm sharing with your mother."

She walks to her room and I hear the scrape of plastic against the hardwood floor.

After Dad left, Mom took down most of the pictures in the house because he was in them. She said it hurt too much to look at them. Now our walls have bright spots where sunshine didn't fade the paint because a picture of us used to be there.

Mom put some of Grammy's things in the plastic tub holding those pictures. It's sort of like a memory box now. But nobody looks at it. I guess some people want to remember and can't, and some people remember and don't want to.

I hear Grammy shuffle through the papers and picture frames. Finally, she emerges with a little square, cut out from a magazine and glued to an index card. The edges are frayed, and it's all yellow and faded. But there's a recipe on it. The same secret recipe Grammy never shared with Mom, no matter how much she asked.

Maybe this is all a big mistake. Will Mom be mad to have the magic cookies she wasn't ever able to make herself?

Grammy starts mixing, and I stay close by. I know how fast she can forget what she's doing, and I doubt magic cookies will be quite so magical if they're burned black.

Grammy keeps saying, "I'm going to show you. These magic cookies. They'll do the trick. You'll see."

"But how will they help? What will the magic do?"

Grammy wipes her hands on her apron. "Well, we won't know that until we give the magic away."

"Then how do you know it will help?" I still remember all the times Grammy made those cookies and wouldn't share the recipe with Mom. Mom wouldn't eat even one. Dad said she was only punishing herself and ate all of them. I think that made Mom even madder.

"I just do," says Grammy. "Because I believe." She turns on the oven light. "Now you sit here and observe and tell me if it isn't magic."

As I watch the balls of dough go from gooey blobs to crumbly cookies, I admit that it does look a bit like magic. But even if there is magic, there's probably not enough to make Mom forget to ask me if I'm going to sing in the presentation. And I definitely don't want to tell her I'm not, and see that disappointed look on her face, or hear how much she misses hearing me sing. She was so happy this morning when she thought the music might be coming back.

I focus extra hard on watching the cookies bake so I don't have to think about it.

Mom walks in right after the fourth batch is out of the oven. She stops in the doorway like she's run into a wall. "Who's baking?"

I throw two cookies on a small plate and carry it over, trying to get the magic to her as fast as possible, before she has a chance to talk about school.

"Peanut-butter cookies," I say, holding the plate out.

"Pat's peanut-butter cookies?"

I nod and push the plate into her stomach so she has to take them. "Try one, Mom. They're really good."

"I know they are." She takes the plate but doesn't eat anything. Instead, she carries it over to the counter, where Grammy is spooning more dough onto another cookie sheet. Mom picks up a warm cookie, flicks off some crumbs, and turns it over to look at the other side. "It looks perfect like always." But her voice doesn't sound like she really thinks it's perfect.

She finally takes a bite. A tiny one. A nibble. Is it enough magic? If there really are such things as magic cookies, she probably needs to eat a whole one. But she doesn't. She puts the cookie down, stares at the counter, and gasps. "Pat, is this what I think it is?"

Grammy turns around. When she sees the magazine clipping with the recipe on it she freezes.

"Is this your peanut-butter cookie recipe?" Mom asks.

Grammy slowly wipes her hands on her apron. She looks at the recipe and then at me. She doesn't look at Mom at all as she says, "Yes. I . . . um . . . thought it was time to pull it out again." She mumbles something, then, "Pass it on," and more mumbles.

Mom lays the piece of paper on the counter and reads the whole thing from start to finish. "All this time, I've been racking my brains to get my hands on this recipe," she whispers. "It was in a magazine."

"Not just any magazine," Grammy huffs. "*Better Homes and Gardens*."

"Why?" asks Mom.

"Have you ever opened a *Better Homes and Gardens*? They have recipes in every issue."

"No. Why are you giving it to me? I've been asking for it for years. Last time I asked, you said you'd die before you told me. I believed you."

Grammy slides the cookie tray in the oven, sets the timer, and slowly walks around the counter to where Mom is standing. "Family is family, Elizabeth."

They're the same words Mom said when Grammy moved in with us. When Mom said them, it sounded like a duty. But when Grammy says them, it feels like the other half of a two-way promise.

Mom puts her hand over her heart and whispers, "Thank you."

After dinner, Grammy sits at the table with a plate of peanut-butter cookies and doesn't move. I finish drying a plate and say, "What's wrong, Grammy?"

She sighs. "It just doesn't seem right to have peanut-butter cookies without making some music."

I put the plate away. "I thought you never wanted to do that again. Remember?"

"What?" gasps Grammy. "I love making music. Don't you remember all those times I played with my Tony? I love it."

"But you said . . ." I stop. Grammy doesn't remember yelling at Dad and telling him she's sick of playing the piano and hates singing with him. She doesn't remember how he was already so sad by that point that he hardly smiled, or how after that, he never smiled.

A hard, tiny piece of anger that I'd been carrying around with me finally melts away. Because I understand now. She wasn't the real Grammy when she said those mean things. She was already forgetting. Her anger was to cover up her embarrassment.

I want to tell her that I forgive her, but if I say that, I'll have to remind her about what happened a year ago, and I don't want to do that. When your brain can't hold all its memories, you should only keep the good ones. Instead I ask, "Do you want to play the piano right now?"

"Oh, Kate." She picks up a peanut-butter cookie. "I'm not sure my hands remember how."

"I'll help." I turn around and Mom is standing in the kitchen doorway. She's holding the songbook with the cover falling off. "I know it's not the same having me play. But it doesn't feel right without music, does it?"

Mom sits next to Grammy at the piano. She curls her fingers over the keys. "You want to try, Pat?"

"No, dear. I'm good."

Mom doesn't ask me to sing with her. She just starts playing an old Beatles song. I tense up as she finishes the intro, nervous to hear the music without Dad or me singing along. Worried how it will make Mom feel. How it will make me feel. But in the space where there's supposed to be words and singing, a different sound fills the room.

Whistling.

Grammy is whistling the tune instead of singing. "My eyes are so bad I can't read the dang words anymore," she says between the first and second verse.

Part of me wants to join in, mix my guitar and voice with the piano and whistling like the butter, sugar, and eggs in Grammy's recipe. A couple times, I even take a deep breath and open my mouth. But nothing comes out because the thought of singing makes my throat ache, and I don't want to ruin the moment with tears. The music still wraps around me like a blanket, though. I curl up on the leather recliner and just listen without feeling guilty that I can't sing along.

By the end of the night, the plate of cookies is empty, the house is full of music . . . and I finally know the magic is real.

*Dear Dad,*

*I wish you could see Grammy now, see her forgetting. Maybe you'd come home. Maybe, before all her memories are gone, you could have one last night of music and cookies.*

*And maybe that would make you happy again.*

*Love,*

*Kate*

# Chapter 17

*I* can't sleep. All I can do is think about Everyday Magic and that it's real. I want to shout about the magic, and jump on my bed, and run around and give it to everyone. But it's past my bedtime, so I can't.

Instead, I decide to get a drink of water.

As I creep past Mom's room, I peek in her door and see her turning her cell phone over and over in her hands.

I push the door open a crack more. "You should call him."

Mom drops the phone like it's a billion degrees. "Oh, Katydid. You scared me."

I lean my head against the doorway and say it again so she can't pretend she didn't hear. "You should call Dad."

"No, I don't think that would be a good idea."

When it was time for me to break my first board, Sensei wrapped my hand and fingers in tape and told me to visualize breaking the board over and over. And then to strike hard and fast, and most importantly, to trust that he would hold the board completely still for me. Sometimes talking with Mom about Dad is like breaking that first board all over again. And so I visualize and visualize. But a part of me can't shake the feeling that she's not holding the board perfectly still.

"What if he's waiting?" I ask. "What if he just wants to know we want him home? What if he really needs some peanut-butter cookies?"

"Katydid." Mom's hair falls into her face. "*He* left *us*. Not the other way around."

"But maybe he—"

"No." Mom stands up and walks to the door. "Katydid, no. He asked us to leave him alone."

But I know Dad wasn't thinking about peanut-butter cookies when he told Mom that, or he would have made an exception.

When I go back to my room, I spot the Harrises' orange cat prowling around our bushes. I watch him slink between shadows and light, his dusty orange fur against the gravel. My fingers itch for something warm and fuzzy to cuddle.

The first note of *Pathétique* crashes through the house. It sends a shaking through my body that makes my hands clench into fists. I throw open the window, lean my head outside and feel the cool breeze on my neck.

"Fred," I call. "Here, kitty, kitty." He jumps up onto my window ledge, purrs as I scratch behind his ears, and then hops down, disappearing back into the orchard.

I sit on my bed, my insides still filled with the shaking and the up-and-down motion of the piano music. There's no way I can sleep through this. I grab a piece of paper and dump my box of colored pencils onto my bed. After scattering them around, I find the orange one, twirl it in my hands for a moment, and start drawing.

My hands don't move like Jane's. She makes it look easy. Like drawing is just a bunch of quick strokes and dashes that all of a sudden form into a picture of something. I can't draw like that. I have to go slowly, carefully. I close my eyes and imagine Fred. The orange face and orange eyes. The way his ears flick at every noise.

I stop drawing to examine the face on the paper.

It looks pretty awful, but I keep going anyway. Maybe I just need to color it in. First the bright orange like a sunset. Then the yellowish stripes.

I stop.

It's not quite right.

Maybe some red. I add red around the yellow stripes.

Now it looks even worse.

I groan and pick up the whole piece of paper, ready to throw it away. But then a thought pops into my head. What would Jane do with this picture? It's not hard to come up with an answer. I pull out each colored pencil and add more stripes. Blue stripes, pink stripes, purple stripes, until my picture is no longer of an orange tabby cat, but a rainbow cat. The kind of cat Jane would love.

I gently fold it up and put it in my backpack just as Mom plays the last notes of *Pathétique*.

♪ ♪ ♪

*Dear Dad,*
*Sometimes I wonder why we say you're the one with depression when Mom and I are the ones being flattened into the ground.*
*Kate*

# Chapter 18

*I*n the morning, when I get to school, I search for Jane to give her the picture. But I notice Sofia first. She isn't standing with Marisa. She's sitting next to the wall by herself. I don't know what's going on, but I can't let an opportunity like this go to waste.

I sit down by her, my backpack scraping against the wall. "Hi."

"Oh, hi, Kate." Sofia squirms a little before settling back into her crisscross-applesauce position. The purple patch over her knee points toward me.

"Where's Marisa?"

"She has a dentist appointment."

"Cool."

Sofia's eyes dart back and forth between me and the ground. "I'm really sorry I told Marisa about your grandma. I didn't know it was a secret, or I swear I wouldn't have told."

I sigh. "I know."

"How is she?" Sofia asks, leaning forward so she can see my face better. "Your Grammy."

"She's good." While we talk, everything inside of me feels like a cup of hot chocolate. "You should come and see her. Say hello." Sofia opens her mouth to respond, but I rush on before she can say no. "I know you have *Annie* rehearsals today. But maybe on Saturday or Sunday. What do you think?"

"That sounds nice."

That hot-cocoa feeling inside me keeps building. I let part of it out by clicking the toes of my orange tennis shoes together. "I've missed you, you know."

Sofia leans back against the wall. "I know."

I'm sure she's about to say it, too. It has to be there in her heart just aching to come out. But instead, the bell rings. "Oh, better go in," says Sofia.

She gets up and leaves me there with all my words sitting and flopping on the ground, like a fish gasping for air.

She didn't say she missed me, too. Was that on purpose? Or did she just forget?

A hand reaches down. It's Jane. She stuffs a piece of paper into her back pocket and helps me up. "Going to school today?"

"I guess."

She's still wearing the orange hat I gave her. "Nice hat," I say.

Jane taps it. "I love it. Parker told me you made it! That's so cool."

"Yeah." Then I remember the picture from last night. I swing my backpack off my shoulders and pull it out. "I drew this. I thought maybe . . ."

Jane unfolds it like she's ripping open the wrapping paper on a birthday present. She stares at it for a minute before breaking into a huge smile and turning the picture around. "This is totally what I'd look like as a cat."

"It's not as good as what you can do."

Jane shrugs. "It's just a different style is all. More geometric."

"It has lots of mistakes."

"That's what makes it art," replies Jane. "My mom says that if something looks perfect, it's not really art. You might as well just take a photograph and not waste all that time. And she would know. She went to art school."

For a second I wonder if Jane would say the same thing about mistakes if she could see my life. Would she call it art?

♪ ♪ ♪

We walk in the doors and put our backpacks in our lockers. Right before we enter the classroom Jane adds, "So are you still feeling good about karate for the presentation?"

Sofia waves at me from her desk, and for a moment I wonder if singing would make everything between us the way it used to be again, instead of being as tricky and frustrating as bar chords.

*I laid my pointer finger down as flat and as hard as I could over the guitar strings. My tongue stuck out of my mouth in concentration. Deep breath. Placing my other fingers where they were supposed to go, I closed my eyes. I'd been working on playing this bar chord for three weeks. My hand shook from pushing down so hard. I lifted my pick into the air like a magic wand and strummed the strings.*

*The guitar buzzed, half the notes coming out tinny and wrong.*

*"Dang it!" I yelled, pushing my guitar off my lap and onto*

*the floor. It fell with a crash that echoed with music. I turned to Dad sitting on the couch. He was going to kill me, treating my guitar like that.*

*He was looking at me, but his face didn't change. He didn't move, or flinch, or say one word.*

*I picked up my guitar from the ground, watching him, and wondered for a moment if he could hear or see me at all.*

"Yes," I tell Jane. "Karate is perfect."

"Great," says Jane. She leans her head to the side. "So . . . want to come to my house after school? We can make our presentation super awesome, eat cookies, all that stuff."

I freeze.

"I can't," I whisper.

Because that's when it hits me. Cookies . . . peanut-butter cookies . . . magic. The magic is how I'll make everything go back to the way it used to be with Sofia.

# Chapter 19

*I* eat lunch with Jane, Brooklyn, and Emma again, because I don't want to mess anything else up with Sofia before I give her the magic. In class, we had put the finishing touches on our poem, and over lunch Jane and I talk about how I'll use karate moves in our presentation. Our ninja George Washington jokes weren't that far off. It will probably be pretty silly, but at least I won't be singing.

When school gets out, I run home as fast as I can. Past the crossing guard and Mr. Harris's almond orchard, waving bees away from my face the whole way. I throw open the door to the house.

"Ssssh." Mrs. Harris dashes out of the living room and motions for me to be quiet. "I just got Amelie down." She stands on her tiptoes to look behind me and out the front door. "Where's Parker?"

"Parker?" I'd forgotten Parker. In all my thoughts about magic and Sofia, I forgot that Parker would be walking this way.

He gets to the door a few seconds later, breathing heavy. "I couldn't catch up."

"Sorry."

"It's okay." He holds out a book for me. "I found this for you at home and thought you might like it."

I take it from him. The cover has a picture of two knitting needles and a ball of yarn with the words *59 Ways to Cast On and Bind Off.*

"Thanks," I say, flipping open the book. "I'm really new to knitting, though."

"Oh," says Parker. "I can take it back. I just thought—"

"No, it's okay." I remember what I'd told Parker when he saw my hat. "I bet it will help when I teach you how to knit."

I hold my breath to see if he remembers, if he still thinks that would be fun.

Parker grins. "Awesome."

A high-pitched cry comes from the other room. Mrs. Harris sighs. "There's our cue, buddy. Let's get going."

As soon as they leave, I toss the book on the hall table and rush into Dad's office.

Grammy's lying in bed, but sits up when I say, "Tell me about the magic again."

"Is that baby gone yet?" she whispers.

"Amelie? Yeah, they just left."

Grammy puts her hand over her heart. "Gracious, I have never seen such a colicky baby before. Of course I lucked out with your father. He was the happiest baby in the world, I tell you."

I brush away her comment about Dad and push my hands into the mattress, leaning closer to Grammy. "Tell me about the magic."

"The magic? What magic?"

No. It's not a good time for Grammy to fade away. I need her right here. "Everyday Magic," I say, slower this time. "Like you gave to your friend when you kissed that boy and she forgave you. I need it. How did you do it?"

"Oh, you mean the gum-wrapper necklace?"

"Yes!" I yell.

"Oh, my. You're certainly excited today. What do you want to know about it?"

"How did you make it? How'd you make the necklace magical?"

Grammy points to the door. "Bring me my bag and I'll show you."

I go out to the hall, grab the bag, and bring it back. Grammy's propped some pillows up behind herself. She rummages down at the very bottom of the bag for a couple minutes before saying, "Ah, there it is," and pulling out a small pack of gum with three pieces left in it. Her face looks like she's not holding gum, but diamonds. Magic gum is probably better than diamonds anyway.

"Now watch carefully." She takes a piece, unwraps it, and pops it in her mouth. As she chews, she folds the wrapper up into a little V shape. I watch the whole time but I'm not very good at folding things.

"Show me again."

Grammy doesn't say anything. She just does it again, and then again a third time. After she makes three of the V's, she shows me how they hook together to make a chain.

I bounce on my tiptoes. "But what about the magic?"

"What about it?"

"Well, how do you put it in there?"

Grammy sets the tiny chain on her lap and touches my cheek. "I don't do anything to make this chain magical. When you make something for someone else, you give them love they can hold. That's where the magic comes from. Anytime love becomes visible, there's magic. You can't stop it or take it away or add more. It's just there."

She picks the chain back up. "But this won't do anyone any good. We need more gum." Grammy gets out of bed, grabs her jacket off the dresser, and says, "Let's go to the store."

"The store?" My stomach tightens. "Mom doesn't like me to leave the house by myself."

"Oh, what your mother doesn't know won't hurt her," she says with a laugh and a wave of her hand. "Plus, you won't be alone. I'll be with you."

Sensei's voice comes into my head. *You must weigh all of your options and then proceed swiftly and with purpose.*

I know by now that having Grammy around doesn't always mean I'm not alone. She could take off down some path in her mind and not be back for hours. But if I'm going to get Sofia to be my best friend again for sure and for always, I need more magic gum wrappers. Sofia's words come back to me. *It never hurts to try everything. Not when it's important.*

I grab my Christmas money and we leave.

We walk to the end of the road and catch the bus at the stop in front of the school. It drives us past Mr. Harris's almond orchard, the onion fields, and what will be a watermelon patch when summer comes, before turning left and heading into town.

Even in town, an orchard or small farm will appear between buildings. Mom says our little city is spreading out and taking over more land that used to grow things. But sometimes it seems as if the rich, dark earth is creeping into the city, settling down somewhere, and then deciding to break out into great big fields of lettuce and tomatoes.

The bus drives us all the way across town to Walmart. We only have an hour before Mom gets home, so I go straight to a checkout line. But Grammy shuffles past me.

"Grammy, where are you going?" I grab three packages of gum and chase after her.

She makes a turn into the office supplies and stops in front of a huge shelf of notebooks in every color.

"Come on, Grammy. Let's go."

She touches the cover of one of the notebooks. "Roses are red, violets are blue, write a poem in this book, to say I love you."

Her voice is wrong. I grab her arm. I can't lose her this far away from home. "Grammy. Pat. It's me, Kate."

"Kate. I . . . I need this notebook for my poetry. Poetry for Alice."

I tug on her sleeve and look up and down the aisle, hoping maybe someone will show up who can help me. "No, we came for gum. Come on, Grammy. Let's go."

"We love writing poems back and forth," she whispers. "It's what friends do, you know. It's kind of like magic."

She isn't really standing in the Walmart anymore. She's standing somewhere a long time ago. But she still knows about the magic. And the notebooks are only ninety-seven cents. I grab a bright orange one and take her hand. "Come on, Grammy. Let's go."

For a second, she doesn't move, and all I can hear is the

blood rushing behind my ears. But finally she follows me to a checkout line beside a rack of sunglasses and candy. Below the boxes of spearmint gum is a package of sparkly colored pens.

"Oh, Jane would—" Something catches my eye then. I don't know what it is, but it's like my brain just knows something's important. I search for the thing that made my insides snap to attention. Then I see it, three aisles over. A green baseball cap with the letter *A* on it and a red stain on the brim. I know that hat, and I know the only person in this whole Giants-loving town who wears it.

Dad.

I want to shout and run up and hug him. But I shove those feelings so deep down inside my stomach I have to crouch to hold them in. I make a little squeak as I duck behind the candy racks.

"Oh, no," says Grammy. Her mouth lifts out of that puckered frown, and I know she's back. "What's wrong? Are you hurt?"

"It's Dad," I whisper.

"My Tony?" She stands on her tiptoes and looks around. "Where?"

"Over there in the A's hat."

Grammy throws out her arms. "Let's go say hi."

I shake my head and slowly straighten up, careful not to turn around, so Dad won't recognize me. "No."

After months of asking Mom where he is, when I actually have the chance to talk to Dad, all I can hear are her words coming out of my mouth. "He doesn't want to see us."

"Now that's just silly," says Grammy. "Of course he wants to see you! If I know my Tony, and I think I do—I *am* his mother—then he'll want to see you."

My heart stretches. But it snaps when I remember
what Mom said last night. How *Dad* left *us*. Not the other
way around. "No. Mom said he needs time away from . . .
everything. That means us."

It's my turn to check out. The cashier taps her lime green
nails against the metal at the end of the conveyor belt. I hand
the gum and notebook to her.

"Pish posh," says Grammy. "I'm going to give my Tony a hug."

I whirl around to grab her arm, but she's already pushing
past the people and carts behind us, muttering. "Of course he'll
want to—" Her voice gets quiet then. Almost a whisper. "Tony?"

That's when I know she saw his face.

I pay the cashier and run straight for the door. I don't wait
for Grammy. I almost forget my bag. But I have to get outside.
I have to breathe cold air and sunshine and stop thinking,
thinking, thinking about Dad's face.

# Chapter 20

*I*t smells like cows. Like grass and rain and mud all pressed together in a heap. Still, I breathe deep and fill my lungs. Then I sit at the picnic table where we always used to eat enchiladas from the food truck. But I don't think about enchiladas, because then I would have to think about Dad, and I'm trying to think about cows.

"Cows, cows, cows," I whisper.

I pull the hood of my jacket up over my face just as Grammy walks out the door. She sniffles as she sits next to me, so close that I almost fall off the bench.

"That's not my Tony."

"Yes it is."

"But what happened to him? His hair, that beard . . . his eyes. He looks hollow and lost." She stares at me as if I'm the grown-up and she's the kid.

"It's the depression," I say. "One day the sadness came, and it never left."

"My poor Tony."

Then Dad walks out of the store.

I pull my hood even further over my face so he won't see me, won't recognize me. But I should know better. He hasn't seen me for five months and nineteen days, and even before he left he didn't *really* see me. He just walked around with that lost look. All this time, I've only wanted Dad back. But now that I know he's still sad, still scruffy and empty, I want to hide. I don't want him to look at me and not see me.

But I've spent over five months wondering where he is. So when Dad gets to the street and turns right, I stand up and start walking.

"What are you doing?" asks Grammy.

"I'm following him."

Grammy nods and comes with me. We don't run. We stay far back like spies.

He turns onto another street. "I just want to see where he's going," I say.

But I want to see other things, too. Like if Dad has a new family, or if he's by himself. If he still stays in his bedroom all day, or if he's out doing all the fun things we used to do together. If he misses us. If he wishes he were home.

We turn down the same street as Dad, trailing him past a long row of bushes right to the end of the road, where he enters a huge, brown apartment building.

As we walk up to the list of names and apartment numbers outside the doors, a lady with a screaming baby rushes past us.

"There he is," says Grammy. "Apartment 304."

I can't help looking around me and wrinkling my nose. How could Dad leave our house to live in this gross apartment building with weeds growing in the cracks of the sidewalk and stinky ashtrays out front?

"Well, we know where he lives," says Grammy. "So now we can . . ." She looks at me and waits for me to finish the sentence, to give her a plan.

"Go home," I say. "Let's go home."

There's a quiet space where the wind blows between us and carries away all the words I wish I'd said instead.

"My poor Tony."

"At least now we can mail your letter."

Grammy doesn't hear me. She's staring at the ugly building. Finally, she says, "Do you think he needs me?"

I nod. "And me. And Mom."

"And magic," she whispers.

"And magic. Can we give him some?"

"Yes. If you love someone you can always give them magic. And you always should. We never give up on people we love. I know that better than most."

We go back to the store, hop on the bus, and then walk as fast as we can from my school to home. The closer we get, though, the further Grammy disappears. She keeps saying things like, "Now where are we? Where are we going? This doesn't look familiar."

"Almost there, Grammy," I whisper, holding her hand.

Mom pulls into the driveway just as we're walking up the front steps. I don't have time to hide the plastic grocery bag. I'm trying everything I can to get Grammy to go inside.

"No, where are you taking me? This isn't my house."

Mom gets out of the car. "What's going on? Is everything

okay?" Then she sees the grocery bag. "Did you go to the store?"

"Grammy, this is where you live now," I say. "I'll show you your bed and all your things."

Grammy shakes her head and pulls her hand away. "No. No."

"Did you go to the store with her?" Mom asks again.

"We were safe," I say. "I know how to get there."

Mom walks up to the door. "It's not you I'm worried about, Katydid."

"Don't call me Katydid!"

"Excuse me?" She says it in that voice that wants to see if I'm brave enough to say it again.

I'm not.

Mom turns away from me. She puts a hand on Grammy's back and rubs in circles. "Pat, let's go inside and make some hot tea. Then you can go home."

"Okay," she whimpers.

Mom leads her into the kitchen like a little kid. As she puts the teapot on the stove she says, "You're lucky she didn't do this to you at the store. Or on the bus. What if you couldn't get her here?"

I let those questions float right out the screen door without bothering to catch them or answer.

Grammy shifts in her chair and hums nervously.

"I'm coming, Pat," Mom says before turning to me. "So what's in the bag?"

I hand it off to her.

"Bubblegum?" Mom pulls out one of the packages. "You know how I feel about bubblegum."

"It's for Sofia."

"Sofia? Why?"

"I'm making her a necklace out of the wrappers. So we'll stop fighting and be best friends again. Just like we used to be."

Mom sighs. "Oh, Katydid."

"What?" I grab the bag and the gum back from Mom so she's standing in the kitchen with her hands out in front of her but nothing in them. They hang there for a minute before she slowly places them on my shoulders.

"Do you know the hardest part about running Mayor Gerton's campaigns?"

I groan. "Not again."

Mom puts her finger to her lips. "No. Listen." She bends down so she's looking me straight in the eyes, so she knows what she's about to say will really go in. "You can give the voters all the information in the world. And you can even drive them to the polls. But in the end, you can't force them to vote for your candidate."

I push her hands off my shoulders. "What does that even mean?"

"It means . . ." Mom takes a step back and waves her hand in the air. "Wouldn't you rather make this necklace for Jane?"

"Jane?" Her name echoes off the kitchen cabinets and bounces around inside my brain. I look into my bag at the bright colors of gum and the orange notebook. A rainbow in a grocery bag.

"Yes, Jane. She sent you a text today."

"Liz?" Grammy says like it's a question. "Liz?"

Mom hands me the phone and hurries to Grammy. I find her text messages. Under the number I recognize as Jane's it says, *Hi Mrs. Mitchell, this is Jane. Kate's partner on a project at school. I'm sending these texts for her. OK?*

The next text reads, *Kate, do you feel ready for our presentation tomorrow? Maybe we should get together tonight and make sure we're good to go. The switch from singing to karate has me nervous.*

I quickly text back. *Can't. Too busy. And I've got the karate down. Don't worry.*

Then, before Mom comes back, I flick down to find the last message I sent Dad. Merry Christmas. It still says it's unread.

When Mom finishes helping Grammy, I hand the phone back. She reads what I texted Jane, sighs, and pulls the box of herbal tea from the cupboard. "Don't you think you'd like to get out of this house for a little? Play with someone?"

"Play?"

Mom rolls her eyes. "Hang out. You know, with somebody other than Sofia. Maybe it's time to, I don't know, try new things."

"I don't want to try new things."

Mom takes a tea bag from the box and places it in Grammy's mug. "Katydid, sometimes friends grow apart. And that's okay. It's part of growing up. I know it hurts. I remember when—"

"It's just been a few misunderstandings, Mom," I say, stopping her from trying to talk about our feelings. "And, you know, Marisa and the play. It's not . . . nothing is changing." It comes out louder than it should.

"Things are always changing, honey."

I stomp my foot. "Not this!"

I run to my room, drop the grocery bag on the floor, and walk over to my guitar. I pull the polishing rag out and sit down on my bed, running it over and over the dark wood until it shines.

"There," I whisper. "Soon." Because it's real now. Dad, Sofia, the magic. It's all real. And it's all happening.

♪ ♪ ♪

*Dear Dad,*

*Have you ever wanted anything so much you could actually see it? The first few days after you left I swore I saw headlights pulling into our driveway every night because I wanted to see them so bad. And now that I know the magic is real, now that I know it works, I can see Sofia sitting in my bedroom talking about school and homework and everything.*

*And I can see you too. Driving up, walking in, coming home.*

*Love,*

*Kate*

# Chapter 21

*I*t's five thirty when I wake up. My body must know it's an important day. The day magic will change everything for me. I flip on my light switch and pull out the necklace and the notebook.

The necklace is perfect, all shiny and silver. Jane would probably love it. She needs something silver to wear. But it isn't for Jane. I need to remember that.

I hold the notebook on my lap, fish around under the bed for the shoebox, remove the sparkly purple pen, and try to think of a really good poem. Something with magic. Something to win back and keep a best friend. But the only poem that comes to me is the one Grammy said at the store.

*Roses are red, violets are blue, write a poem in this notebook, to say I love you.*

I change the last line to try to make the magic work exactly how I want it to.

---

*Roses are red, violets are blue, write a poem in this notebook, because that's what best friends do.*

Right as I close the notebook, Grammy tiptoes in and sits on my bed. She has her knitting and needles with her again. I wonder if she always knits before the sun's awake.

"We saw my Tony yesterday, didn't we?"

I nod.

"He didn't look good . . . did he?"

I shake my head.

Grammy sighs. "I'd been hoping I could blame it on this rotten noggin of mine."

All at once, I want to make her smile, really smile, the way she used to before she was sick. When every time she looked at me she knew who I was. "I'm giving him magic today," I whisper. "I'm taking him all his favorite things: peanut-butter cookies and ice cream and spaghetti."

"And a hat?"

I don't have time to make a hat. "I don't know."

"My Tony needs a hat. He's scared and sad. He needs a hat to keep the bad thoughts away." Her hands slip on the needles as she struggles with a stitch. "Gosh darn it."

Grammy is absolutely right. Dad needs a hat. But she isn't going to finish it. She's making knots and dropping stitches.

"Here. Let me help." I take the needles from her and begin my slow, unsure knitting. "Just stay here with me. Tell me stories about Dad."

But Grammy only sits on my bed, staring around my room, getting lost somewhere in her mind. I want to reach inside her, take her hand and pull her back. She whispers, "My Tony."

Maybe he's in there, holding her hand down one of those windy paths. Suddenly, I feel like the loneliest person in the world.

At seven thirty, Mom knocks on my bedroom door. She walks in and sees me knitting again. "Big day today," she says. "How are you feeling about that presentation?"

I'd forgotten about the presentation in all of the magic. Somehow, George Washington doesn't seem as important as a dad and a best friend. So I put on a smile and tell an almost-lie.

"Good. Great."

"Wonderful! I can't wait to hear all about it, Katydid."

I bristle at the insect name.

As soon as Mom and Grammy leave, I shove the necklace, notebook, knitting, and shopping list in my backpack. Then I notice Grammy's letter. It's lying near the top of my shoebox full of notes. Dad's name is still on it with nothing underneath. I stuff it in with everything else and run into the kitchen. Since I don't know how much spaghetti and ice cream will cost, I need some more money, just in case my Christmas money isn't enough. Fortunately, I know exactly where to get it.

Mom's in her room still getting ready, so I sneak some bills from the emergency fund. I know that it's for super emergencies, like forest fires and tornadoes. But we don't live by a forest. And we don't get tornadoes. I guess we could have an earthquake, but if I have a dad again it won't matter if the whole house shakes to the ground.

I grab some peanut-butter cookies, too. Hopefully the magic didn't wear off while they sat in the cookie jar. But even though my backpack is filled with magic, it still feels too light. It's not enough. Something is missing, and I can't have anything missing. With something as important as this, I have to try everything.

I wander out of the kitchen, through the living room, into the music room, looking, looking, looking. And then I see Dad's guitar case with his freshly polished guitar inside, right where I left it.

That's it.

That's the last part of the magic. Mom comes out of the bedroom right as I'm picking up the case. It's a little heavier than I remember and the end of it swings, hitting the wall.

"What are you doing, Katydid?"

I freeze. "I'm, uh . . ." I can't tell Mom my secret plan to take Dad the magic. She'll tell me I can't go.

"Is that for your presentation today?" Her face breaks out into a bigger smile than I've seen her wear in a long time. "Are you going to sing?"

A thousand beetles crawl across my chest when I tell the lie. "Yep."

Mom rushes over and scoops me into a hug, sending the guitar case bumping into the wall again. "Oh, I'm so happy. I'm so, so happy." She pulls away and wipes at her eyes. "I can't wait to sing with you again, Katydid."

I hope that after today Mom won't ever call me that again. But I don't mention it. Instead I say, "I can't wait to sing all together again, either." It's the biggest truth I've told in a long time.

I grab an apple off the counter and run for the door, a little lopsidedly because of the guitar. Knowing I have all that magic in my backpack waiting to be given away makes me feel like a firework ready to shoot into the sky.

"Whoa! What's the rush?"

I open the door. The sun pours onto my skin. "It's a huge day."

Mom laughs. "You know, I think you're right."

I look out into Mr. Harris's orchard and see the blossoms

fluttering off the trees and I just know, know, know. Today everything changes.

Then I'm gone, running right into that change so big it's all I can see.

I have to keep switching the guitar from hand to hand because my arms get tired, but I still race past the orchard, past the crossing guard, all the way to school. I arrive right as a maroon van pulls up and Parker jumps out. I don't know if I should speed up or slow down, because I don't know if I want to talk to him or not. But he sees me and waves.

"Hi, Kate."

"Hi, Parker."

"Did you hear about the rain today?"

I look at the sky and spot a small patch of gray clouds in the distance I hadn't noticed before. "I didn't know it was supposed to rain."

Parker nods. "Loads! My dad has been praying and praying for rain all winter, and it's finally here. But he says it's too late. And this storm's supposed to be big—so big it might rip all the blossoms off the almond trees and destroy the crop. He's really nervous."

Mom's always talking about how California needs more rain. I've seen the signs telling people to pray for it. I never thought it was only a good thing at a certain time. *Aren't good things always good things?*

The magic in my backpack feels heavier. Dad's been gone for five months and twenty days.

What if I'm too late?

I have to try the magic. Now. Just to remind myself that it still really, truly works. I have so much right there in my backpack. It can't hurt to share a little bit with Parker.

I put the guitar on the ground for a second so I can unzip my backpack and grab a peanut-butter cookie. But when I look back to where Parker was just standing, he's gone. Reading and walking, he almost trips on a trash can. The cookie feels stupid and crumbly in my hands.

As I get closer to the front doors, I see Marisa in the middle of a group of girls. Sofia stands to the side.

Holding the cookie a little tighter, I make my way toward her. I'm going as fast as I can. But I don't quite get to Sofia before the bell rings and everybody pushes inside.

Jane comes up next to me as I walk through the front door. "Hey, Kate."

"Oh, hi."

She's holding a big piece of sketch paper, folded in half. "I did the drawing for our presentation today. This isn't it, but . . . is that a guitar? Did you change your mind? Are you singing?"

"No. I'm not singing." It comes out sounding short and prickly. I speed up and try to push closer to Sofia, but Jane stays right by my side.

"*Oookaayy.* So the guitar is just a decoration. Whatever." She points at the cookie in my hand. "What kind of cookie is that? Is that your breakfast? Your mom is so much cooler than mine."

"It's peanut butter. Do you want it?" I mumble, still trying to keep an eye on Sofia's dark ponytail up ahead.

"Sure! Thanks. You know, there's lots of cookies at my house. Not cookies for breakfast obviously, but after-school snack cookies . . . if you want to come over."

I don't even look at her. "I can't. I've got lots to do today."

It's the truth. Right after school I'm going to Dad's apartment and giving him all the magic.

Jane stops walking and grabs my arm so I have to stop, too. "Seriously?"

I can't see Sofia anymore. "I'm sorry. You can still have the cookie, though."

Jane crumples up the piece of paper she's holding and shoves it at me. "Forget it." She weaves into the crowd ahead without even looking back.

People are moving all around me, but I stay still and unfold the paper. It's a picture of two girls. One is holding a pair of knitting needles that are hooked by yarn to a hat on top of the other girl's head. It's me and Jane. My throat feels tight like skin with a sunburn.

As I fold the picture back up, the cookie in my hand breaks apart and falls to the ground. I bend down to pick up the pieces right as someone steps on them and grinds them into the floor. And then all I can do is stare at that. At my cookie. My magic. Broken and stomped on.

I've tried to give the magic away twice already, and it hasn't worked. A voice inside me whispers, *Maybe you're just too late.*

# Chapter 22

*T*he rest of the morning trickles along slower than Bear Creek. The rain clouds rumble in while Parker and his partner, James, give their presentation on Martin Luther King Jr. Parker shows defensive karate moves for a peaceful demonstration, and James plays a protest song on his trumpet.

The sky blackens while Sofia and Marisa give their presentation on Ellen Ochoa, the first Hispanic woman in space. They do a song and dance together, just like I thought they were planning. A few days ago, that might have made me sad. Today, it doesn't matter because all I can do is worry about the magic.

There are two, three, four more presentations before the lunch bell rings. As Miss Reynolds announces that Jane and I will be the next group up after lunch, the wind starts shaking the windows.

At my locker, I grab my sack lunch, the notebook, and the gum-wrapper chain, gently lowering it over my head and touching a few of the links. The rain is coming, and I can't help remembering what Parker said earlier, can't help worrying my magic is too late or not enough.

Grammy's voice whispers in my mind. *Believe.*

Deep breath.

I have to get the magic to Sofia. Then do the presentation. Then help Dad. Everything will be better after that.

I practice exactly what I'm going to say to Sofia as I walk to the cafeteria and wait by the door. Jane sits at her usual round table with Brooklyn and Emma, reading a tiny, wrinkled piece of paper. Parker is still in line. When Sofia takes a seat, Marisa isn't around, so I sit down right next to her.

"Hi," I say.

Sofia straightens up. "Hey." She pokes at her green beans, and my whole planned speech runs out of my head.

Instead I say this: "Do you remember when we stuffed all those green beans and fries into our milk cartons last year?"

Sofia smiles. "And then dumped them in the toilet so it looked like someone threw up?"

"Do you think anyone found that? Do you think they thought someone was actually sick?"

"Eeew!" Sofia giggles. "That was so gross!"

"Yeah. But it was fun."

Sofia stabs a green bean and holds it up on her fork. "Yeah, it was."

I pull the chain off my neck and hold it out for her. The silver links hang below my hand. "I made this for you."

Sofia touches one of the wrappers. "Wow," she whispers. "You really made that? That's a lot of gum!"

136

"Yep. It's for you. It means we'll always be friends." I push the notebook across the table. "And I have this for writing poems and stuff."

Sofia looks toward the lunch line and then flips open the notebook and reads the poem on the first page. After slowly closing the notebook, she taps on the cover. She's silent a long moment before sighing and saying, "Thanks, Kate. Do you think . . . maybe . . . Marisa could do it with us?"

"What?" I practically choke. "No. This is just for us. For best friends. Me and you."

Sofia picks up the notebook and looks at the cover for a few seconds before finally saying, "Then . . . I can't take it."

"Why not?"

"Well . . ." She looks back to the line, and I know who she's looking for. "It would hurt Marisa's feelings if I had a notebook all about how you and I are best friends."

"But I thought *we* were . . ." My throat aches too much to finish.

"We were." Sofia puts the notebook down with shaky hands. "I mean, we are. It's just . . . Marisa is my best friend, too. You're . . . both my best friends."

That's when I spot her new necklace. A gold chain with half a heart on it. And I realize, finally realize, Sofia's moved to a new orchard. She's sunk her roots down deep and isn't leaving.

"Liar," I whisper.

"What?" Sofia's eyes get squishy and wet like she cares what I have to say. But I know it's just one great big dopey act. Like when she'll be on stage in *Annie*, pretending to be a sad orphan, while she has a mom and a dad right there in the audience, waiting to bring her flowers and scoop her up after the show.

"You're not best friends with both of us. If you were best friends with both of us, then you'd spend time with both of us. But . . ." My voice catches. "You're always with Marisa."

"That's just because of *Annie*."

"And sleeping over at Marisa's house on the weekends and partnering up for everything in class."

"When *Annie* is over, we'll hang out again. I promise."

The space behind my eyes is hot, and the burning pushes all the angry words out of my mouth. "Don't promise. I hate promises. I hate them!" I stand up so fast the whole table shakes. "Real best friends don't have to go back to being best friends. They never stop to begin with."

Outside, the first raindrops slip down the windowpane. I throw my gum-wrapper chain across the floor and run out of the cafeteria. I race to my locker, grab my backpack and the guitar, and I'm out the door, on the playground, at the bus stop. By the time the bus comes, I'm completely soaked by thousands of great big drops of too-late rain.

♪  ♪  ♪

*Dear Dad,*

*I'm writing this to you on the bus. I couldn't stay at school. Sofia isn't my best friend anymore. Things will never go back to how they used to be with her. But I still have you. You need me and I'm on my way.*

*I'm missing the presentation and I don't care. Because you are more important than George Washington.*

*Love,*
*Kate*

# Chapter 23

*T*he grocery store was full of staring eyes and the hollow sound of my footsteps. But standing in front of Dad's door with a sack of groceries in one hand and a guitar in the other is scarier. My arms are stretching and pulling out of shape with the weight. The paint on the fake wood door is chipping, and the number 304 hangs crooked and lopsided.

I take a few shaky breaths and try to form my arms into that strong, rounded position that always comes before the kata at karate. But the bag and guitar are too heavy.

I knock. Long and hard. It echoes in my brain. Deep and shaking like the thunder rolling outside. Then I wait.

He doesn't come. And he doesn't come. And he doesn't come.

My whole body is like a bike tire with a tiny hole leaking air. But I'm not leaking air. I'm leaking hope, lots of it, until the knob finally turns and the door opens. Dad stands behind it, staring down at me.

I saw him yesterday. But I guess part of me hoped he'd answer the door and be my old Dad again. Because when his face is still saggy and scruffy, I'm surprised.

"Hi, Dad," I whisper.

He scratches his cheek and that scraggly beard sounds like soap on the cheese grater when Mom makes laundry detergent. "Katydid."

I think it's how he says it that hurts the most. Like it's a question. Like he's not sure.

"What are you doing here?"

That hurts second worst.

"I followed you yesterday. I know I shouldn't have, but I saw you at the store and I couldn't help it. So I'm here and . . ." When I hear myself, it doesn't sound right. But the thunder booms again, and I know I don't have time to explain. I walk straight in with big steps. Powerful steps. Steps carrying magic.

Dad moves out of the way. "What's in the bag?"

"Food. And I brought this." I lean the guitar against the counter, put the bag next to it, and take Grammy's letter out of my backpack.

"My guitar," he murmurs. "Why?"

I push the envelope into his hand. "Because I want to help you. I want to make you happy again. And Grammy wrote you this letter. It's all magic."

"I don't . . ." he mumbles as he rubs his hair. "I told your mom I didn't want anyone coming by."

That hurts more than getting kicked in the thigh when I miss my block in karate.

"You didn't really mean it."

Dad nods his head and walks into what must be the living room. The whole apartment is so small and cramped I can't tell for sure. There's a little gray fold-up chair and our card table from back home. I didn't realize he'd taken it until I see it there. Dad sits down and opens the letter. I figure that means I can cook. So I do.

I pull out pots, fill one with water, and open spaghetti sauce jars. The moving and cooking and following directions pushes the hurt part of my heart out of the way. I'm busy. You can't feel too sad when you're busy. Dad needs me to make the most perfect spaghetti, and that's what I'm doing until I hear his bedroom door close.

"Oh, no," I whisper. He can't go back into the bedroom. Not today. Not now.

Something on the card table catches my eye. The letter from Grammy. I walk over to pick up the envelope and the pages underneath.

"No."

Grammy sent a letter to Dad but forgot the most important part. She sent him five blank pages.

"Oh, Grammy." I thought the letter would be something to make that magic called forgiveness. But there's not much magic in just an envelope with Dad's name on it and plain white computer paper.

The water on the stove isn't boiling yet, so I turn the heat down on the sauce and pull the guitar out of its case. I know what happens when Dad goes into his bedroom, how he pulls the blankets over himself and doesn't move. I have to get him the magic before he starts staring too hard at the wall. Before he's too far down that road, and I can't bring him back.

I push the door to his room open. It smells funny. There are clothes everywhere and garbage on the floor. It isn't clean like at our house. But he lies on the bed just the same, looking out the window. When Dad is sick like this, he's too tired to clean up or get dressed, or do much of anything else.

I march to where Dad's looking and sit down. So instead of looking at the window, he has to look at me. He has to see me. And because I don't know what else to say, I prop the guitar up on my lap, curl my left hand around the neck, and start playing.

The thick steel strings cut into my fingers. Almost six months without playing has weakened the skin there. But I keep going, my fingertips brushing each string up, one, two, three, four, in an arpeggio and then back down.

His breathing is slow and steady.

As I finish the intro, I worry that after so many months, my singing voice might be screechy as a blue jay's. But instead, those first few notes come up my throat and out my mouth soft and smooth. They spread through my chest like ripples in a pond. They fill up the room with something alive and real. With hope.

*"Where are you going, and what do you wish?*
*The old moon asked the three."*

Dad rubs his cheek against the pillow.

I sing, and I sing, and I sing. It's as if I never stopped. Like I'm returning home after a long trip. Even here in this dingy, dirty apartment with stinking piles of clothes all over the floor. Because I'm making music with my dad and that's where I'm from. This is who I am.

I end the song and close my eyes as the last vibrations fade away. Dad's voice is dry as paper. "Katydid."

I've waited five months and twenty days to hear Dad say my name again, to say it like he knows me for real and forever, and when he does, it's like somebody shaking up a root beer and pouring it over ice. All the foam comes spilling out from inside of me. "Daddy, please come home. Please come home. I can make you happy again. Mom will understand. I know you're sad. But I'm sad too. And Mom's sad. She needs you. *We* need you."

It feels as if I'm finally resolving a chord that's been dissonant for too long. But my words just bounce off of him. All the fizzy foam sinks down, down, until there's nothing left.

"Please?" I whisper.

And then just like Grammy, his eyes clear for a moment. He's walking out of that misty, winding darkness. "Katydid, I love you."

"I love you, too, Dad." I reach for his hand and link my fingers between his. For a moment I think it's working. The music and the spaghetti and the ice cream—it's working. But then everything changes.

Dad straightens his fingers and slips his hand away from me. He pulls his blankets up around his shoulders and rolls over to face the wall.

It's Dad's way of saying it's over. He has more important things to do. Like nothing. Like staring at a closet. Like making everyone around him feel invisible.

He's done.

I have to get out of that room. That room with the stink and the inky invisibility swirling all around me.

I run into the kitchen. The sauce is bubbling. There are red splotches on the stove. The water is boiling. The ice cream is melting into a puddle on the counter.

But I don't care. I don't care about anything.

"I'm not cleaning up," I shout back to the bedroom. "This is your mess. Not mine, not Mom's, not Grammy's, yours!"

I shut the stove off, put on my backpack, then grab Grammy's letter from the card table because Dad doesn't deserve it.

I leave the guitar, though. I never want to see it again.

On my way out, I slam the door. Loudly. But he probably doesn't even hear it.

The rain is pounding when I get outside. I run to the bus stop and then ride past the grocery store and the onion fields to the school. Halfway home, next to the orchard, I see Mom's car. It speeds down the road, stopping on the opposite side with a screech like one of those radio sound effects.

"Where have you been?" Mom jumps out, leaving the door wide open. Without even looking for other cars, she runs across the street to me and grabs my shoulders. Her mascara is smeared under her eyes. "The school said you didn't come back from lunch. I've been looking all over for you. Where were you?"

I can't think of a single lie. Not one. All I can think about are the white petals squashed into the mud around us and all those almonds that will never grow now. "I found him," I say. "I found Dad and I tried to make him happy. I tried, but . . ."

"Oh, honey."

I don't say anything else and neither does Mom, because sometimes the only thing you can do is stand on the side of an orchard and cry as the rain washes away the last of your magic.

Part III
Trust

# Chapter 24

**W**hen we get back to the house, Mom wraps me in thick blue towels and gently squeezes the water from my hair. Her touch is so soft, it seems like she's trying to dry away every bad thing that's happened in the whole last year. Water drips from all over me and pools around my feet.

Then I sit next to Grammy, knitting on the couch with a different set of needles. Red metal ones.

"I tried to give him the magic," I whisper. "Dad. I took him so much. But it didn't work. There was . . . no magic. Not in any of it."

Grammy adds a few stitches in her knitting, shakes her head and pulls them out.

I want her to look at me and tell me that the magic is still real. That this must have been a huge mistake and maybe there's a third rule for Everyday Magic and it's that it never works on the first try. I want her to quiet the thoughts in my head saying it's all a big lie. But she doesn't. So I say, "I took your letter, too."

"My letter?"

I nod but don't tell her that she forgot to write anything.

"I don't remember writing a letter."

I guess she wouldn't, would she?

Jane sends me a text and Mom shows it to me. *Where were you today? Are you OK?*

I don't write back.

I don't sleep well.

I don't wake up early. Not for knitting or research or staring at the orchard. I don't want to think about singing or Sofia or Dad. I don't want to ever get out of bed again. Sort of like Dad, I guess. But Mom forces me to crawl out and tells me I have to go to school. I don't know why she couldn't do that with him.

At school, Jane stops me outside the classroom, her arms folded. "Where were you yesterday? You missed our presentation!"

"Oh . . . I was . . ." I shrug. I don't want to tell her.

Jane's shoulders slump. "We only get graded together. Miss Reynolds says we can make it up this afternoon. So are you ready to do . . . whatever with your karate?"

"Yeah," I mumble. "Sorry."

Jane nods and stares at the floor. "It's okay. Just warn me next time you decide to disappear. I'll put up fliers with a reward or something."

I smile. "Will I get the reward if I turn myself in?"

"Yes," replies Jane. "The reward of my brains helping us get a good grade."

"Works for me."

In the middle of math, I raise my hand. "Miss Reynolds, can I use the bathroom?"

"Marisa already has the hall pass."

Of course she does. Marisa has Sofia. She has the hall pass. She has everything I need. I shut my eyes tight and put my hand on my head. "Please?"

I must sound sick or something. "Okay. Go ahead," Miss Reynolds replies.

I slip out the door and open my locker, not really looking for anything, just trying to take some time to breathe. My backpack hangs open and I pull on it to glance inside. Grammy's knitting needles and the blue ball of yarn topple out and onto the ground with a clatter and a bounce.

"Shoot," I whisper as I bend down to pick them up.

When I stand, Marisa is there holding out the orange notebook I gave to Sofia yesterday.

"This is yours," she says. "I'm giving it back."

I move the ball of yarn to my elbow and clasp the knitting needles between both hands. "It's Sofia's."

"She doesn't want it."

We both stand there and stare at each other. Finally, Marisa says, "It's not my fault. I didn't do anything wrong, you know."

I tighten my grip on the knitting needles. "Really? How would you like it if I came along and stole your best friend?"

"That's exactly what you're trying to do!"

"I can't steal her from you." My knuckles are white around the knitting needles. "She was my friend first!"

Marisa's voice gets higher. "You don't understand her like I do."

"Yes, I do!" I scream. I want to shake Marisa as hard as I can. To grab her so that my fingers sink deep into her arm and then—

CRACK.

Grammy's knitting needles break in two between my hands. Marisa's mouth falls open.

The ball of yarn falls to the ground.

I drop the splintered, useless, broken pieces of magic.

All of a sudden, I forget everything Sensei ever said about self-control. Something inside me snaps like those knitting needles. My fingers curl into claws and a strange noise escapes my throat as I yell, "Look what you made me do! Those were my Grammy's knitting needles!" I run straight into Marisa, knocking her to the ground and landing on top of her with an "Oof."

"It's not my fault! Get off!"

But I don't get off because the anger is pouring out of me now. "She made my dad's baby booties with those. They were supposed to make him better. You stupid, pink—"

I have lots more to say but I don't get to. Someone locks their arms beneath my shoulders and drags me away.

"Kate Mitchell, what on earth?" It's Miss Reynolds. "I've never in all my years . . . I never expected you of all people."

I still want to spit and yell and tell Marisa to get up so I can push her again, but Miss Reynolds's hands are so tight around my arms, I can't.

By the time we get to the principal's office, I don't feel fiery hot anymore. I'm cold, like a shrinking piece of dry ice on a picnic table. The whole time I wait, it sinks in more and more what I just did. All I can think about is Sensei, and what he'll say when he hears I lashed out at Marisa.

*An unprovoked attack is an act of cowardice.*

I hold my head in my hands. Coward. Weak.

Principal Warner finally opens the door and motions for me to come in. She sits down behind her desk. I take the only other chair, set out for bad kids like me. It has a big cushion that's basically quicksand when I sit down.

"I've never seen you in here before," says Principal Warner.

I rub my hands on my pants and don't say anything. The clock on the wall ticks off the seconds of silence.

"Do you have an explanation for your actions?"

What grown-ups call a good explanation and what kids call a good explanation are totally different things. I keep my mouth closed and stare at her ugly pink nail polish.

"Well, Miss Reynolds informed me there were some extenuating circumstances. It sounds like your classmate broke something special of yours?"

I don't look up. Instead, I shake my head. "I broke them." When I say the words I know they're true. Marisa didn't make me do anything. I broke Grammy's knitting needles. Left them lying in pieces in the hall. They were full of her memories and now they're gone.

"I was so mad . . . I just . . . It's all my fault." I have to clear my throat to stop from crying.

"I see. While I appreciate your honesty Kate, we have a strict zero tolerance policy at this school. So, I'm sorry. You will be suspended for the rest of the day."

The words bounce off me like paper airplanes. Go home? Good. I don't want to be here anymore anyway.

Principal Warner smooths her hands over her desk. "We couldn't get ahold of your mother, so we called your father. He's on his way."

Those words roar louder in my mind than a jet flying right through the room. "My dad? He answered? He's actually coming?"

Principal Warner frowns and picks up a folder with my name written on the tab. "Yes, your father. Tony Mitchell, 555-0128, 423 Cabrera, Apartment 304."

My head gets dizzy. I lean back, way back, into that sinking cushion. "You know where he lives? How do you know where he lives?"

"Kate, I don't understand. Should I not have called your father? Your mother listed him as an emergency contact, but if something has changed, you need to let me know."

I shake my head, but all I can think is: *Mom.*

She wrote down Dad's address on that piece of paper. She knows his address! How long has she known? How long has she told me she didn't know where Dad went, when all along she knew exactly where he was? We could have been taking him cookies and making him happy. Instead he sat in that dirty, smelly, dark apartment without us. All because Mom kept telling me she didn't know where he was!

Principal Warner shocks me out of my anger. "Well, he should be here shortly. You're only suspended for the rest of the day. Fighting, no matter . . ."

Blah, blah, blah. She keeps saying a bunch of stuff, but I don't hear it. I feel like one of the butterflies always hovering around the lavender bush. Dad's going to see me and take me home. He'll see the weeds in the driveway. Maybe they'll drive him so crazy that he'll stay to pull them. Then he'll remember. He'll remember how much he misses us and how much we need him.

"Do you understand?" asks Principal Warner.

I nod because I understand the most important thing of all: my dad is coming. Everything will be all right, no matter what Mom has done. No matter how much she's lied to me.

I don't need to understand anything else. Somehow, even though I'd begun to doubt it, the magic worked.

Principal Warner opens the door. "You may sit in the waiting area."

I jump up so fast my knees knock into her desk. "Thank you, Principal Warner."

She looks like it's been a long time since anyone thanked her for punishing them, but I mean it. "Well . . . you're welcome, Kate."

# Chapter 25

*I*t takes forever for Dad to get to the school. Before he does, Miss Reynolds brings me my backpack, the orange notebook, blue yarn, and broken knitting needles. I don't want to think about any of that right now, so I stuff them down to the bottom of my backpack where I can't see them anymore.

While I wait, I begin to wonder which Dad will pick me up. The Dad full of sunshine and music and ice-cream sundaes? Or the Dad from yesterday. The clock on the wall tick-tocks like a metronome.

*The metronome clicked out the beat. Tap, tap, tap, tap. I closed my eyes, took a deep breath, and started playing. My left hand found the frets easily, sliding into the next chord and the next. I didn't even need to look. I could just feel where to go.*

*Muscle memory. That's what Mom called it.*

But when it was time to play the F-major-7 chord, I stuck my tongue between my teeth, and smashed my fingers down as hard and tight as I could. The steel bit into my skin. I ran my right thumb over the strings as slowly as possible. Hoping and waiting for perfect.

And it happened. The most beautiful bar chord ever. Without a single mistake in it.

I stopped playing right there. "Dad, I did it! I did it! I played a bar chord."

He was sitting on the edge of the black leather recliner, staring at the floor. He didn't say anything.

"I'm a real guitar player now, Dad! Did you hear it?"

"Mmmmmm."

*Tap, tap, tap, tap* go my knees. That won't be the version of Dad who comes today. It can't be. That Dad wouldn't come to school.

And then I finally see him. His hair stands up on one side, but he came! That has to mean something. That has to mean he's a little bit better. Dad pushes through the doors and walks right past me, up to Miss Williams. After signing some papers, he turns around and whispers, "Let's go."

I can't help it. I run up and hug him right there. Last night, I thought I'd never see my dad again, and now he's here.

"Okay." He pats my head and then pushes me off, as if I'm the one who's scraggly. Or maybe nobody's hugged him in a long time, which makes me want to do it more. But I don't.

We load into Dad's small red hatchback. It's dirty and stinky, too. But right that second, everything smells fresh to me. Like after a rainstorm. Like hope and answered prayers and new plants sprouting.

Dad starts the car and backs out of the parking space.

"I called your mom. She's going to meet us at your house."

Your house. Not our house. If you could fill balloons with hope and carry them around like a bouquet, then one of mine just popped.

"I need to . . . talk to her about something. Could you maybe stay in your room while I do?"

Talking could be good. That thought fills a new hope balloon as I steal Dad's phone, sliding it off the console next to his seat and into my pocket.

When we pull into the driveway, I leap out of the car as fast as I can and run inside. Mom's already home, and I have a secret plan. I learned a trick two years ago when Sofia's cousin lived with her for a summer and we wanted to spy on her.

Mom always leaves her cell phone on the counter when she comes in. So I call Mom from Dad's phone. Then, before it makes a sound, I answer her phone and mute Dad's. I slide Mom's phone toward the edge of the counter, near the kitchen table where she sits. I have a walkie-talkie and Mom has no idea.

Mom clasps a steaming purple mug in front of her and drums her fingers on it, the way she always does when she's thinking. Seeing her makes all that anger from the principal's office come back.

"You knew where he lived," I say. "You knew this whole time."

I thought maybe she'd try to lie or tell me I was wrong, but she just says, "Is he coming in?"

"He says he needs to talk to you. Probably about being lonely and sad because we never visited him."

"Katydid—"

Dad walks in the door, and Mom shoots up out of her seat. "Tony."

Dad acts like it isn't his home anymore. Like he's a guest waiting for someone to ask him inside. "Elizabeth."

"Come in."

That's when Grammy walks out of Dad's office. She's lifting her gold bag over her shoulder when she sees him and gasps. "Tony?"

"Mom? What are you doing here?"

She rushes to Dad and hugs him. "I live here now. Isn't that nice?"

Dad gives Grammy a short side hug before turning to Mom. "How long has she been here?"

"About a week and a half. She needed some help and—"

"Why didn't you tell me?"

I'd grown so sick of Mom's excuses for not calling Dad that I never thought to ask her if she'd told him about Grammy living with us.

I can't believe I forgot.

Now that he's standing here in the kitchen, filling up space and replacing memories with realness, all of my anger at her *no*s comes spilling out. "You haven't told him yet?" I shout. "You wouldn't even call him for that?"

Mom puts her hands out. "Whoa. I'm not the bad guy here."

"I should have been part of this decision," Dad says.

"Oh, Tony. Calm down," says Grammy. "It's a nice thing she's doing, really. But I've missed you."

And I know this is it. This is all Dad needs. Grammy's here, and he'll see how sick she is and realize she didn't mean it when he asked to play a song with her and she sat at the piano, staring at the music and the keys before shouting, "This is ridiculous. I hate playing this song and I hate making music with you! Don't ask me to do it again!"

Maybe she'll even ask him to play a song with her tonight. But that doesn't happen.

Dad shakes his head and sidesteps Grammy. "I . . . I should have . . . I could have taken her. You didn't have to do this."

"I know I didn't have to," says Mom. "But family is family, and heaven knows you can barely take care of yourself."

Dad's face twists like Mom dropped a brick on his toe.

Grammy blinks. "Ouch, Liz."

"I'm sorry," says Mom, stepping away from the table. "You're right. I should have involved you. But maybe we could discuss this . . . alone?"

Dad nods at me. "Katydid?" Then at Grammy. "Mom? Do you think we could get some privacy?"

I look from him to Mom, and I just know this is like one of those movies where everyone has a big fight and then everything gets patched up and goes back to happy. Things started off kind of shaky with the whole Grammy thing, but that only means we're about to be a bigger family when it's all done.

"Of course," says Grammy. "In a jiffy." She takes my hand and walks me back to my bedroom.

"He wants to talk!" I say as Grammy closes the door behind us. "That's a good thing, right?"

She sits on my bed and pulls a skein of yarn from her bag. "Don't count your chickens before they hatch, Kate."

But it's too late. I've already counted chickens and eggs, and my hopes are higher than a hot-air balloon. I pull the phone out of my pocket and wave it in the air. "I made a walkie-talkie. Want to listen?"

Grammy begins rolling her yarn into a ball. "Of course. Bring that little eavesdropping device right over here."

I sit down next to her and put the phone on speaker,

holding it a few inches from our faces as mom's voice crackles out of it. "How have you been?"

"Fine."

"Fine!" I whisper. "Do you hear that? He's fine! That's better than sad."

"Sshhh!" says Grammy.

"You wanted to talk?" Mom asks.

A chair scrapes against the floor. Mom just sat down. Or Dad did. Maybe both. "Kate came to visit me yesterday."

"I . . . I know."

"Did you . . ."

"No, I didn't tell her to. I didn't even know until after."

"Made me spaghetti sauce and sang to me . . ."

"Tony, I'm sorry. I told her you wanted to be alone."

"No, it's okay."

I swing my feet in the air. "It's the magic. It's working."

"It made me realize something . . . important."

Grammy starts swinging her feet, too. "I think maybe you're right."

Dad's coming back, I can tell. I've been waiting and dreaming and filling hope balloons just for this and here it is.

"I want a divorce."

*Divorce.* It's the ugliest word I've ever heard.

Just like that, my hope balloons all explode.

Grammy drops her yarn. "No, no, no. He doesn't mean that."

"What?" says Mom.

"Kate took care of me yesterday. She did a better job at being a parent in one hour than I've done my entire life. It's time . . . you're better off without . . . someone like me."

"That's not true. You know that's not true. You are a wonderful—"

"Don't blow sunshine, Liz."

"If you would get some help. Just see someone. I know you'd feel better and you'd—"

"Why can't you accept me the way I am?"

"Because this isn't you. Tony, this is not the man I married."

"Which is why I'm asking for the divorce." A chair scrapes again, and I know he's standing up. "I'll send the papers."

"Tony, it doesn't have to be like this."

"I'm sorry."

I can't move. I can't breathe. I can't do anything but listen to Dad telling Mom I made him decide to leave us. Me! And spaghetti and singing. He doesn't want to be my dad anymore.

"Did he really just say that?" I whisper to Grammy. "Divorce?"

"Oh, no," she replies. "Oh, no, no, no. We must have heard wrong."

"I don't think so."

I drop the phone and run out of the room. He's not going to leave, disappearing without a goodbye. Not again. I'm not going to wake up tomorrow morning with everything changed and no dad like last time. I have to make him see, have to make him understand. I have to make him say goodbye.

But I'm too late. Dad's already in his car and driving away. I look at Mom. She's staring at the table like maybe Dad left a message on it.

"This is your fault!" I yell. "This is all your fault. He NEEDED us and you wouldn't let us help. *'No, no, no. Don't get your hopes up!'* I hate you! I hate you!" I run back into my room and throw myself on the bed.

Grammy's still sitting there, but her hands are filled up

with yarn from the ball that she's now unraveling. "Oh, it's just not right. It's not right. Look at this mess. I'm sorry, Kate. I made this huge mess."

I can tell she's lost. But I don't help her. All I can do is curl up into a ball and remember. Why do I have to remember?

When Dad left the first time, I was awake. I could hear Mom and Dad in the hallway.

*"At least say goodbye," Mom said.*

*"What good will that do?"*

*"You're going to break her heart."*

*There was a pause and a sigh. "She's sleeping." His footsteps clomped to the door. It opened. His car started. He drove away.*

I used to think if I'd known that was the last time I'd see Dad, I would have chased after his car. I've dreamed about it hundreds of times. Running after him down the road, right past Mr. Harris's almond trees. They were filled up with nuts and leaves then. I would have run all the way to the end of the trees. And Dad would've stopped and turned around, because you can't ignore someone who runs through an entire orchard for you. You just can't.

# Chapter 26

"Oh, Kate. Someone's coming. Someone's coming. Help me clean this up. I don't want anyone to see me like this."

I lift my forehead off my knees. "Nobody's coming, Grammy. Don't worry."

"I can hear it. It's getting louder. Oh, look at this mess." Grammy frantically gathers loose yarn into her lap, winds it around the ball, knots it even worse.

I listen and wait. Sure enough, the growl of Dad's car is getting louder, not quieter. He's coming back and I didn't even have to chase after him.

I jump out of bed, scoop the phone off the ground, and slide across the tile hallway as I run out of my bedroom. "He's back!" I shout. "He's coming back."

Mom's eyes are pink as peaches. "What?"

I look out the screen door as Dad's car pulls into the driveway. "He's here. He's not leaving."

Mom stands but still keeps one hand on the table, like it's holding her up.

Grammy walks out of my bedroom with yarn in her arms and trailing behind her. "Oh, I'm such a mess, such a mess. Don't let anyone see me like this." She shuffles into Dad's office and closes the door.

Then Dad walks back in. Without knocking, or waiting. Like he lives here.

It's really like a movie now, where everything seems lost, and right when you think there's no happy ending, the hero realizes he made a big mistake and returns. Dad's still scraggly and sad, but now it's in a handsome way. I know he's going to march across that kitchen, grab Mom around the waist, lean her back, and give her a big kiss. Just like the movies. Just like he used to. We'll all cry and talk, and he'll never, ever leave again.

But Dad doesn't do any of that. He stands there with his hands in his pockets, frozen.

I wait for the kiss and *I love yous*. But when Dad opens his mouth, all that comes out is "I left my phone."

I stare down at that ugly black rectangle and then back up at him. "Don't go, Dad."

He puts out his hand. Not asking to hold *my* hand, but waiting for his stupid phone. I put it in his palm just as gentle as I can, but I can't let go of it. I squeeze it until my knuckles turn white. I visualize crushing it like a stupid, empty soda can.

But phones don't break so easy, I guess. At least, not when you want them to.

"Please," I whisper.

Dad's fingers close around the phone, touching mine as they do. They're cold, and I let go.

He puts his hand on my shoulder. "Goodbye, Katydid." And then he walks out the door.

For weeks after Dad left the first time, we kept finding things he left behind. There were cologne traces, footprints on the tile, lost shoes.

There won't be any of those things this time. He's really gone.

Mom falls back into her chair. She can't stand there, holding herself up any longer.

Grammy comes out of her bedroom without her yarn. She wipes her hands on her dress and says, "Tony? I was thinking." She looks around the kitchen at me and Mom. "Where did he go?"

That's when I hear the weird gasping thing Mom does when she's trying not to cry.

I escape back to my room and lie on my bed again.

*"Please," I begged at the door to his room. My guitar was already strapped around my neck. I ran my thumb over the strings. "Will you come sing with me, Dad? It's not the same without you."*

*His room was dark.*

*He lay on his bed.*

*He didn't move or say anything.*

*He was gone the next day.*

I try to think of something else. Anything else. I try to remember happy times. Try to imagine Dad here with me. But there's nothing but that dark room, and the silence, and that question. *Will you come sing with me?*

♪ ♪ ♪

*Dear ~~Dad~~ Tony,*

*Mom says that sometimes when something hurts super bad, your body stops feeling it. I think thoughts can be the same way, and my brain is trying to protect me. It won't let me imagine you here with me, singing, getting ice cream. I can't picture it. That's how I know you really aren't coming back.*

*Does that mean you aren't my dad anymore?*
*Kate*

# Chapter 27

*I* lie there for a long time. The sky turns orange and red, and my back starts aching. I sit up, rubbing at my eyes. They're sore and swollen. My guitar leans up against my bed. There's so much sadness in me, I guess it wants to come out, because without really thinking, I pick up the guitar.

Cradle it like a baby.

Put my fingers on the strings and try to sing. My voice is wobbly, but I keep going.

*"And some folks thought 'twas a dream they dreamed*
*Of sailing that beautiful sea."*

I close my eyes and imagine all the bits of sadness spiraling out of me like tiny threads of spider silk.

*"Wynken and Blynken are two little eyes*
*And Nod is a weary head."*

I stop playing.

What a stupid song. Dad actually sang this to me?

I lie back down on my bed, put the body of the guitar on the ground, and let go of the neck so it falls to the floor with a crash and a twang.

"Oh, my," says Grammy, opening my door. "That didn't sound good." She comes into my bedroom. I can tell by the sound of her footsteps that she's back to herself finally. She always walks a little louder then, like she knows exactly where to put her feet, rather than the shuffling she does when she's lost.

Grammy sits on the edge of my mattress and puts her hand on my head. "Tony's gone, isn't he?"

I roll onto my back, away from her. "You lied to me. There's no such thing as magic."

Grammy pulls her hand away. "What makes you say that?"

"What makes me say that? I gave Dad all the magic I possibly could, and it didn't do anything. It made things worse! I made things worse."

"That's not true," she lies. Again.

"Yes, it is. Didn't you hear him? He left because of spaghetti and singing. That's not magic. That's the opposite of magic. I can't believe I ever believed you."

Grammy sighs and scooches back farther on my bed, trapping my legs against the covers. "I think it's time I teach you the last rule of Everyday Magic."

I roll over to face the wall entirely, just like Dad. "I don't want to hear it."

"Well, I'm going to say it," says Grammy. "So unless you put in some earplugs you're going to hear it. The third rule is a tricky one. It's the reason most people don't believe in magic, you know."

"They're smart," I mutter.

"Trust. You have to trust the magic. That means you can't give it away expecting a certain outcome. You can't put demands on it and say it only worked if everything goes how you wanted it to, or when you wanted it to. Magic has its own timeframe and its own ideas about what should happen. You can hope it will cause some event, but sometimes it will do something else entirely. That doesn't mean it didn't work."

"That doesn't sound like magic. That sounds like what Sofia says about praying."

Grammy pats my arm. "You're a smart girl, Kate. You get that from me, of course."

I sit up. My chest aches so much with all the sad thoughts I've refused to let out for months, that some finally burst free of me. "Grammy, are we still a family?"

"What?"

"Are you and me still family? Dad—no—Tony's gone. He doesn't want me to be his daughter. Does that mean you're not my grandma anymore?"

"No," Grammy whispers strong enough to shoot nails through a wall. "No, no, no." She scoots closer and looks me straight in the eye. "It doesn't matter what your father does or says. I am still your grandma."

Her two dimply hands gobble mine up between them.

"But we're broken," I say. "I tried to fix us and I made everything worse. I made him leave."

"This was not your fault. Don't take that on."

"I cooked him dinner and sang our song. If I'd just stayed away, maybe—"

"Hush," says Grammy. "Tony's decisions are . . ." She stops talking and rubs my hand for a long time. Finally, she looks at me. "Family is family. I love you, no matter what. There's nothing anyone can do to stop that or take it away or add more. It's just there."

I sniff. "That's what you said about Everyday Magic."

"Exactly," whispers Grammy. "Exactly."

I wait for her to go on, to keep trying to put a little bit of something happy and hopeful back into me. "Aren't you going to say it?" I ask.

"Say what?"

"That you think family is a special kind of magic."

Grammy smiles and stares out the window. "Oh, I knew you'd get there on your own."

And even though I don't believe in the magic anymore, it feels good to think about it wrapping around me and Grammy, binding us together forever and ever. No matter where my dad is, or how he feels about me, or what paths Grammy is walking down.

That's when the big, rumbly piano notes from Beethoven's *Pathétique* begin. I growl and roll back over to face the wall.

Grammy takes a deep breath. "I love you, Kate. But someone else in this house loves you, too. Loves you most. She doesn't deserve your anger."

"Mom?" I shake my head. "She lied to me about Dad. She knew where he was and said she didn't. She didn't really want him to come back. If she had, she wouldn't be happy he's divorcing her. She never really loved . . ."

But those notes come even louder through the walls and I can't finish that sentence. It would be the biggest lie I've ever told.

"That doesn't sound like the music of a woman who's happy your father's divorcing her."

And it doesn't. It makes me think about what Dad used to say when Mom played the piano, how he could hear her heart. I can hear her heart right now, and it's crashing and tinkling along with the notes, grinding up into a million tiny pieces.

"What am I supposed to say?"

"You might not have to say anything. Maybe she just needs some magic."

"I don't believe in magic."

Grammy shrugs. "Forgiveness then. Can you believe in that?"

I don't know if I can, but I still walk out of my room and into the music room. Mom is rocking back and forth on the piano bench. The notes have changed to light ups and downs in one hand with the shaking deep ones in the other.

I clear my throat. Mom doesn't hear me. I don't have anything to say anyway, so I sit down next to her on the piano bench.

She doesn't stop playing. That's Mom. She always has to finish the whole song so her body can breathe that big sigh at the very end. When all the music has poured out of her, she pulls her hands back and puts them in her lap. The air around me still vibrates with sadness and anger.

"You're too old for Katydid, aren't you?" Mom whispers.

I didn't expect to hear that in a hundred million years. Mom pulls a piece of my hair behind my ear. "Yes, you're much more of a Kate now. I can see that." She sighs. "Why does everything always have to change?"

She isn't talking about me anymore.

I still don't know what to say so I lean my head on her shoulder, but that's all Mom needs. "I'm sorry for . . . everything. For not telling you where your dad went. He asked me not to, Kate. Not to contact him or visit him or help him. I barely got him to keep the cell phone in case you needed to get ahold of him in an emergency, or just to say hi. But he . . . he didn't want any part of this life anymore.

"I didn't tell him about Pat because I wanted him to come back for the right reasons, not some misplaced sense of duty. I thought . . . I guess I hoped . . . that after a little while, if we really honored his wishes, maybe he'd . . ." Mom leans her cheek on top of my head. Her right hand goes back up to the piano keys and plunks the first few notes of "Für Elise." A high, soft wobbling. Back and forth and back.

"Mostly, I'm sorry I wasn't good enough to begin with. I couldn't make the marriage work. Now I've failed you and him and myself. I tried so hard and it was . . . I don't know." She spreads her fingers out wide and plays the first chord of *Pathétique*. Not loud and booming, though. Instead it's soft and barely there. "Do you know why I play this song so much these days?"

I shake my head and don't say anything. Because I know this is Mom being her own therapist.

"I played this for a recital when I was in high school. It took months to memorize, but I did it. When the recital came I made a mistake and skipped eight pages of it. Eight pages." Mom shakes her head. "I felt like such a failure. But do you know what my parents told me?"

"What?" I whisper.

"They said the recital wasn't the important part. The important part was learning the music, and I'd done that. Even if it looked like a failure on the outside, it wasn't." Mom pulls her hands back from the keys. "I keep hoping that they'd say the same thing this time. That I'm not a failure. That I learned the music. But I just don't know."

Mom's parents died a long time ago. So I say it instead. "You're not a failure."

Mom rubs her cheek against my head. "You're right. I still have you, and that's a pretty good thing I did, right?"

"*I* think so."

Mom chuckles and puts her hands back on the piano. "There's a second movement to *Pathétique*, you know. Want to hear it?"

I nod, and Mom begins to play.

The second movement isn't anything like the first. It's soft and slow and beautiful. Instead of making my insides all shaky, it makes them warm and light. Like I'm just about to peek over a hill and see a sunrise.

I don't know how long I sit next to Mom on that piano bench, or how long she plays this part of *Pathétique*. But she plays it over and over until it fills up the house with a sound I've been waiting to hear for a long, long time. Hope.

I never say I'm sorry for yelling, and Mom doesn't say anything else about Dad. But somehow we both know it's going to be okay. That we're okay. Beethoven wrote a song for that, and Mom knows how to play it.

I know how to hear it and feel it, so maybe I'll be okay, too.

# Chapter 28

Dear Dad,

I only thought about you once today, when Mom and I sat on the porch looking at the stars. Mom started crying. She tried to hide it, but I could tell.

I started humming "Rainy Days and Mondays" because I know that's one of her favorite songs and favorite songs make everyone feel better.

In a few minutes, she was singing along but changed the word Mondays to Saturdays. Then we were both laughing and somehow crying at the same time. Which was weird.

You know what else was weird? I didn't feel weak when I cried. I felt stronger.

It made me glad I left your guitar at your apartment. Maybe you should start singing again.

Love,
Kate

# Chapter 29

On Sunday, the sun streams through the branches of the almond orchard and into my window. Usually that makes me wake with a smile. But today, today I can't get out of bed. Today the bed is swallowing me whole. The sadness of Dad never coming back feels like someone sitting on my chest, pushing me deeper and deeper into the mattress. Like I'll never be able to move again.

I cover my eyes to try to block out the light. I remind myself of ice cream and karate, but all I can see and hear and taste is that sadness, that knowing that everything is different and I can't change it. I can't change it.

And then I think of Dad. Of the months he spent in his room, hardly ever coming out. The way he stared at the wall and did nothing, nothing, nothing. I grab at my chest because it feels like I can't breathe. I can't become sick like Dad. I can't. But instead of getting up, I just start crying.

Mom rushes into my room. "Kate? What's wrong? What happened?"

I throw my arm over my eyes. "I'm like Dad," I whisper.

"What?" Mom steps to my bedside.

"I'm like Dad," I say a little louder.

Mom kneels on the floor and puts her hand on my forehead brushing away my hair. "What do you mean?"

"I feel so sad," I say. "So sad, I don't want to get up today. I'm going to be just like Dad. And I don't . . . I don't want . . . that part of him." The words are heavy, sitting on the blankets between us, and I wait to see what Mom will do with them. What she'll do with me, her broken daughter.

"Oh, no. Oh, honey." Mom wraps me up in her arms and holds me like a baby. "Your dad is sick, but that doesn't mean you'll get sick, too."

"You don't know that. You can't know that. Don't lie to me."

Mom's head nods against my hair. "You're right," she says. "You're absolutely right. But I do know this. If something happens and you feel that sadness rolling in, you have something your father doesn't."

"What's that?"

"Sensei."

I pull away and raise an eyebrow at Mom. "Sensei?"

She nods. "What does Mr. Amori say about getting help?"

"The strong man knows when he isn't strong enough," I recite. "He knows when he needs help and he's not afraid to ask for it."

"That's it. You are strong, Kate. Strong enough to get help when you need it. A therapist. Medicine. Your father . . . he's not ready yet. He thinks he doesn't need help. But you." Mom cups my face in her hands. "You are the strongest person I know."

"Really?"

"Really." If words are things that can sit on beds and take up space, then Mom just took my fears and hurled them away, out the window, out from between us. And when she hugs me, I swear my heart is closer to hers than ever before.

Mom sits next to me and pats my leg. "But you know what else would help with that sadness inside you?"

I shake my head so hair falls in my eyes.

"Singing again. That's when things really got bad for your dad. When he stopped singing. It took away . . ." Mom sighs.

"A way to let the sadness out," I finish for her.

"Exactly."

We sit there for a few minutes and watch the sunlight reach farther and farther across the gray carpet.

Finally, I whisper, "Okay. I'm ready. But I've got a lot of work to do."

"Work," Mom laughs. "For what?"

"For my presentation. I'm going to sing."

Mom kisses me on the forehead. "I love you so much, Kate. And maybe you should get in touch with Jane. She's sent me about a hundred texts this weekend."

Mom isn't lying.

*Are you OK?*

*Did you punch Marisa?*

*Are you suspended forever?*

*Brooklyn and Emma missed you at lunch.*

*We're giving our presentation on Monday no matter what. Please say you'll be there.*

*Do you like this picture?*

*Do you need some cookies? My mom made them.*

After I read her texts, I write back. *I'm okay. See you tomorrow for the presentation.*

The rest of the day, I'm glued to Mom's laptop and my guitar, working out the chords and melody for the George Washington "Where I'm From" poem Jane and I wrote together.

Grammy disappears into her room around lunch and doesn't come out the rest of the day. When Mom peeks in on her after dinner, she comes back to me and shrugs. "She's just knitting."

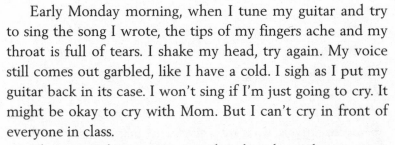

Early Monday morning, when I tune my guitar and try to sing the song I wrote, the tips of my fingers ache and my throat is full of tears. I shake my head, try again. My voice still comes out garbled, like I have a cold. I sigh as I put my guitar back in its case. I won't sing if I'm just going to cry. It might be okay to cry with Mom. But I can't cry in front of everyone in class.

Then something on my window bench catches my eye. It's a pink hat and two wooden knitting needles, just a little bit bigger than the ones I broke. There's a card underneath. It says,

*For Kate,*
*I thought you could use some extra magic for your presentation today, even if you don't believe in it anymore. It was a bear to make this hat, so I think I'm done now. This brain and these hands don't work the way they used to. I guess that makes this my last magic hat. I'm handing off my other pair of wood knitting needles to you because I*

*think you'll change your mind about magic someday. You'll want these when you do.*

*Love,*
*Grammy*

I read that note over and over and then carefully stow the note and the hat in my guitar case. There's something about magic. Even though I don't believe in it, the idea of it, the wanting it to be absolutely, positively true still pulls at all my edges.

Right before I leave for school, Mom gives me a so-tight-I-can't-breathe hug. "No fights today, okay?"

I nod into her shoulder.

"Your presentation is going to be wonderful. I know it."

"It's the magic," says Grammy. "It will work today, Kate."

I can't look at her. I don't want Grammy to see I don't believe her.

When I get to school, I head straight to my locker, hang up my backpack, walk into class, and take my seat without talking to anyone. One by one, everyone else starts wandering in and sitting down. Some of them steal glances at me, some at my guitar. They're thinking about what I did on Friday and wondering what I'm going to do today. Sofia looks at me, then looks away, clutching her books to her chest.

Marisa comes in, and I know what I have to do. Mom practiced it with me this weekend.

Marisa's eyes get wide when I stand up and meet her at her desk. "What do you want?"

Everyone is definitely watching us now. I take a step closer to Marisa for privacy, but she backs away. "I'm sorry," I whisper. "I was wrong. You didn't . . . do anything. I'm really, really sorry."

Marisa doesn't say anything for a moment, just stands there, stiff. Finally, she mutters, "I'm sorry your Grammy's knitting needles broke." Then she sits down, and I head back to my desk, feeling like I just sparred with a ninth-degree black belt.

Parker, who must have come in while I was talking with Marisa, leans over and whispers, "I missed you at karate on Friday."

*Friday.*

I don't even want to think about it. "Yeah, it was a bad day."

Parker nods as if he understands, and I don't need to say anything else. Then he points at my guitar. "I've been waiting four days to hear this."

I roll my eyes. "No, you haven't."

"Technically, I have. It's going to be awesome, isn't it?"

"I don't know."

"It is. It totally is." He settles into his chair and pulls out a thick book, *The Two Towers*, opening it to the first page.

Then Jane is standing in front of me, tapping her pencil on my desk. She sees my guitar and stops. "Are you going to sing?"

"Yes."

"Like really, definitely, for sure?" Jane looks like she doesn't quite believe me. "You don't have to, you know."

"I know I don't have to, but I want to." I take a deep breath. "Sorry about last week."

Jane shrugs. "It's okay. Gave me time to turn my painting into a whole mural."

"Really?"

"No. But I could have."

We stare at each other for a second and then both give a little giggle. "I'm watching you," she whispers, pointing at me. "No fighting. No running away. I mean it."

"Yes, ma'am."

After Miss Reynolds takes us through a math lesson, she stands in front of the class and says, "And now we will have one last 'Where I'm From' presentation. Jane and Kate, the floor is yours."

I carefully unhook the clasps on my guitar case and open it up. When I lift the lid, I see that pink hat again. I don't believe it's magic, but the edges of me are whispering to try it. After all, I need as much help as I can get. I pull that pink hat out and roll it around in my hands.

I don't mind that it's pink, actually. Not anymore. It's a soft pink, like the blankets Parker's mom wraps Amelie in. The promise of something new.

"Kate?" Jane calls. "Are you coming?"

"Yep." I stuff the hat in my pocket and grab the guitar and our poem. Then I march to the front of the room where Jane is already holding a poster painted with the branch of a tree filled with soft pink blossoms all across it.

*"I'm from a myth,"* she reads.
*"From the axe that cut down the cherry tree.*
*From the words never actually spoken*
*That somehow still are true*
*Of me.*
*I cannot tell a lie."*

The whole class claps for a moment, and then everyone is silent when they turn their eyes on me.

I sit down, but don't lift my guitar right away. I touch the hat in my pocket. I want to believe in magic. I *really* do. If believing in magic is like sinking into an ocean, I'm almost totally underwater but my head is still up, gasping for air.

I pull out the hat, ready to put it on. But when I do, Grammy's note flutters out with it. I pick it up and one part catches my eye.

*I think you'll change your mind about magic someday.*

I remember the story about Dad and how he used to believe in magic when he was a little boy.

I know then that I can't wear the hat. No matter how much I want the magic for myself. It's meant for Dad. From the time Grammy began knitting this hat, it was his. Always his, not mine.

I lay the hat and note in my lap, pick up my guitar, and clear my throat. My fingers press against the cold steel strings. My thumb runs over five strings for a perfect C chord. Then all six when I play G. I try to strum that tricky bar chord next but miss it. My guitar buzzes.

I freeze.

Everyone is looking at me. Waiting. Even Sofia, who smiles and nods.

I take a shaky breath and try again. C chord. G chord. F chord . . . fail. The strings crash together with wrong notes.

The corners of my eyes are getting hot and prickly.

Maybe I'm not a real guitar player anymore. Maybe Dad leaving has taken the music out of me. Maybe I'll never get it back, and this aching sadness will never come out.

*Believe*, I hear Grammy saying.

I shake my head and play again. More slowly this time. C chord. G chord. Pause.

Jane puts her hand on my shoulder and gives me one short squeeze.

And then the magic happens.

Real, actual, true Everyday Magic.

I stretch my left hand as wide and flat as it will go. Pressing my pointer finger tight against all the strings, I play F major 7. It comes out true, and in my head I hear Dad saying, *That's when you know.*

And I know. I know, I know, I know.

Somehow that knowing rises out of my chest, through my throat, and out my mouth. The singing doesn't hurt the way I thought it would.

> *"I'm from the grave out back*
> *Holding my dad*
> *Beneath a cross*
> *And a layer of mud.*
> *I'm from the way my mother cries*
> *When she thinks about my father.*
> *The way I try to make him proud*
> *With each battle won.*
> *I'm from feeling like I've failed*
> *Each time I bury*
> *Another son."*

There's silence when I finish. Miss Reynolds takes a step forward. "Kate, that was . . ."

"Amazing!" Jane shouts. "That was amazing!"

And then the rest of the class starts clapping. Even Sofia. Even Marisa.

I'm sitting in that chair with my guitar on my lap waiting to wake up from this dream. But I don't. Because it's real. That bar chord was real. The singing was real. Everyday Magic is real.

♪ ♪ ♪

At lunch, I walk into the cafeteria, thinking about Grammy and her rules of magic. Grammy said that magic happens when love becomes visible, when you give people something they can hold. But I think she was wrong about that, because some things you can't hold, not really. Like a firm squeeze that says it's okay, or a song that makes you feel better. Like a family that's always, always a family no matter what. You can't knit that, or cook it, or draw it, or write it. But all those things are magic.

And Jane gave me some.

I look around for her, and Brooklyn and Emma, but they must have switched tables. Sofia is already eating with Marisa. She gives me a small wave. I wave back. She doesn't ask me to join them and I don't want to. As I walk past, Marisa hands Sofia her favorite kind of granola bar, peanut butter chocolate chip. I wonder what kind of magic that will bring them.

Then I spot Jane and the other girls at a table by the window. Jane has her sketchbook out. I walk up to them and set my lunch bag down. "What are you drawing?"

Jane pushes the sketchbook toward me. "The trees in that orchard over there. I'd rather draw them with blossoms, but . . ." She shrugs, pulls the sketchbook back, and returns to drawing.

I sit down next to her, but I don't say anything. There are too many words buzzing around in my head, and I'm not sure which should come out first.

Jane erases something, growls, and reaches into her pocket. She pulls out a crumpled piece of paper, reads it, and then shows it to me. "Did you know Michelangelo once said this?"

The paper reads, *Genius is eternal patience.*

I shake my head. "What does that mean?"

"My mom says it means that anything good comes with lots of practice and waiting for the right moment." She taps her pencil against the paper and draws a few lines before erasing again. "I think maybe Michelangelo was full of it."

I lean over to see the picture of the orchard trees again. "It looks pretty good to me."

"I don't want it to just look pretty good." She closes the sketchbook and peers at me. "You did a really good job today."

"Yeah," says Emma. "It was awesome."

Brooklyn nods. "It was even cooler than ninja George Washington . . . which is pretty cool."

They all laugh.

"Thanks."

Jane taps her tennis shoes together, one purple and one orange. "I'm glad you sang."

"Me too." I touch the pink hat in my sweatshirt pocket and wonder how on earth I can ever thank Jane for the magic she gave me.

"Is that the hat you pulled out during the presentation?" Jane asks, pointing. "Did you make that one, too?"

"No, my grandma did."

She nods. "Are you going to wear it?"

"No, it's . . ." I don't know how to tell her about my dad and the magic, so I just say, "I don't wear pink. Or, I didn't. I don't know anymore."

"I wear pink," says Jane.

I take the hat out of my pocket, look at Jane, and finally see her. Like she's been in an old, fogged-up mirror all this time and I've just wiped away the steam. "I know. It was a silly tradition."

"With Sofia?"

"Yeah."

"Is the hat for her?"

I can't help glancing to Sofia's table, but it doesn't hurt to see her anymore. "No. She has a new best friend. It's for my dad."

"A pink hat for your dad?" Jane asks.

Emma leans her head to the side like she's trying to understand. Brooklyn stops braiding the bracelet she's making and listens.

"When he was little he was scared, and my Grammy made the hats to help him feel better." I run my fingers over the pink stitches. "He left. My dad. He was too sad to stay. And my grandma can't remember things a lot of the time, not even how to knit anymore. Mom says one day she might forget me . . . forever."

I don't know why I tell them that. They hadn't asked, but somehow I want Jane to know. And Brooklyn and Emma. All of them. I don't want to carry that secret a second longer.

"I'm sorry," Jane whispers.

"Me too."

As I put the hat back in my pocket, it hits me. The perfect way to say thank you for the magic. "Can I come over to your house after school?" I ask Jane.

"Really?"

"If you still want me to."

"What about your sister? Don't you have to watch her?"

I freeze when I remember how I lied to Jane. You can't be best friends with someone and lie to them about having a little sister. They'll find out.

My voice shakes when I say, "I . . . don't have a sister. I

lied. I was nervous about what you would think about my grandma if I had to invite you to my house. I'm sorry."

Jane chews on a strand of her hair for a few long seconds. I know she's going to say she never wants to see me again.

But instead, she tells me, "My mom doesn't really bake cookies. She buys them at the store and heats them up in the microwave and puts them on a plate and has an air freshener that smells like cookies. I lied, too. I'm sorry."

Lying about cookies and lying about a sister seem like two totally different kinds of lies. But maybe there's another part about Everyday Magic that Grammy got wrong. Maybe magic isn't just given away and then a little bit comes back to you. Maybe magic is passed back and forth. I gave Jane magic with the hat. She gave me magic with that shoulder squeeze. I gave her magic when I asked if we could do something together after school. She gave me magic when she didn't get mad at me for lying about having a sister.

We've been trading it back and forth for days. Because that's what friends do. And that's what magic is for.

"I'll have to call my mom to make sure," I say. "But I know she'll say yes."

"Brooklyn, Emma," Jane says. "You guys should come too."

"We can't today," says Emma. "Basketball practice."

Brooklyn nods. "But maybe next time."

"Yeah, next time." Jane opens her sketchbook to her picture of the orchard again. "There's going to be lots of next times."

I look from the sketchbook to the orchard to Jane, and I know she's right.

# Chapter 30

*I*'m super excited about going to Jane's house, but there's one thing I have to do first.

"When your mom picks us up, could we maybe stop by my house and then my dad's apartment?"

We're at our lockers after lunch. Jane carefully turns her dial. "Your dad? I thought he left."

"I know where he lives."

"You need to talk to him?"

"No. Just give him something."

"I can ask my mom, but she'll probably say yes. What are you giving him?"

I pass her the hat.

"Oh, yeah. Do you think it will work like when he was little?"

"I don't know."

She hands the hat back. "That's okay. You have to try everything when it's important, right?"

And suddenly, I'm a tree transplanted between orchards, and I can finally sink my roots down deep into the earth. I can finally feel at home again.

After school, Jane's mom picks us up. First, she takes me to my house. I bolt inside, drop off my guitar, grab the shoebox full of notes from under my bed, and then run back to the van.

I can't seem to get out when we get to Dad's apartment, though. The box of letters is heavy on my lap. Sometimes it's hard to know the right amount of love and the right amount of letting go.

"Is this the place?" Mrs. Chu finally asks.

I nod because my throat's too scratchy to talk.

"I can go with you if you want," says Jane.

"No," I whisper. "I want to go alone."

Jane nods. "Okay. Good luck."

At the door to Dad's building, I turn and wave. Mrs. Chu rolls down the window.

"We'll wait here," she calls.

I run up all three flights of stairs because the elevator is taking too long, and then tiptoe to his door. The numbers are still crooked. He's probably inside lying on the bed, or sitting in his chair, looking at nothing.

I know then I don't want to see him. And really, he doesn't want to see me.

But he still needs a hat. I take it out of my pocket. It isn't beautiful. Grammy dropped some stitches and there are bumps where she tried to pick them back up. It's good enough for keeping out fears though.

I stare at the shoebox of letters in one hand and the hat in the other, wondering what Dad will think when he sees them. Will he understand what I'm giving him? What I'm trying to say?

I sit down, put the hat and shoebox on the floor, and open my backpack. All I need is some paper, but my fingers touch the orange notebook I'd given to Sofia. It's the perfect solution.

I pull out the notebook, open it to the first page, and read the poem I wrote for Sofia.

*Roses are red, violets are blue, write a poem in this notebook, because that's what best friends do.*

After tearing out the page, I start writing to Dad. The words pour out of me faster than a river after spring's snowmelt.

*Dear Dad,*

*I'm leaving you this hat Grammy made and a box of letters I wrote, because they're the most magical things I have to give. Each one holds a little piece of me. A little bit of magic. Family is family, forever and always, no matter what.*

*Love,*

*Kate*

*P.S. I love you.*

I close up the notebook, set it on the shoebox, then put the hat on top. There will be more knitted hats for Dad in the future, since he might need them, and I know how to knit now. But there won't be any more letters. Because I can't keep taking all my hopes and shoving them under my bed. Hope doesn't belong in a shoebox.

When it's important, you try everything. And now I have to trust that the magic will work and make . . . something happen. Perhaps one day, Dad will able to believe and then give.

After I've arranged everything outside his apartment, gentle as an almond blossom, sure as magic, I give three short knocks.

Just before running away, I think maybe I hear the sound of guitar chords floating through the door.

Maybe. Just maybe.

I make my way back down the three flights of stairs and out into the blinding, brilliant sunlight. With one last look at Dad's building, I can't help whispering something between a prayer and a wish for him.

"The magic is real. I promise."

# Acknowledgments

A book is a very special piece of magic, and this one had a lot of it along the way. Thank you to those who

**Believed:** First and foremost, thanks to Rob, who believed in me before I even believed in myself; to Jane, Max, and Tom, who always thought a book deal was around the corner; to my parents, for instilling a love of books and a work ethic that made anything seem possible, and to my sisters, Darci and Kim, who read this book early on, believed in it, and talked to me about it, even when life was incredibly hard. Thanks to Sarah Erickson, for being my first CP and seeing something special in my work; to Peggy Sheridan Jackson, who read the rewrite that changed everything and told me, "This is it." Thanks to Emily Ungar and Jennifer Ray, for being my first fans, and to my Sisters of the Pen: Cindy Baldwin, Ashley Martin, and Jamie Pacton, for the strength that comes from sharing and believing in each other.

**Gave:** This book would not exist if it weren't for Brenda Drake and her contest, Pitch Wars—thank you for giving me a second chance. To my mentors, Joy McCullough, Jessica Vitalis, and Rebecca Wells, thank you for giving more than was required, for taking on a book without reading it, putting me through my paces, and helping me create something beautiful. Thanks to Heather Truett, Rebekah Kritsch, Ellie Terry, Cindy Baldwin, Jamie Pacton, Heidi Stallman, Kit Rosewater, Cory Leonardo, Michael Mammay, Kat Hinkel, Julie Artz, Heather Murphy Capps, Shanna Rogers, Maria Mora and my Pitch Wars 2015 group, who have spent the last three years celebrating and commiserating together, and who helped me make a big decision; to Joanna Thatcher, Kayla McCartney, and Claudia Correa, for keeping my kids cared for and my house clean during the moments of high stress; to Isabel Davis and Kayla Rivera for your thoughts, expertise, and helping me finally understand Sofia and Marisa; and to Joan He, for helping Jane become more real and for writing her that beautiful poem. So many people gave me thoughtful critiques of my work. I'm sorry if I missed anyone.

**Trusted:** Thanks to Sarah Gerton, who pulled my book out of the slush and passed it along; to my agent, Elizabeth Harding, who never stopped believing, giving, and trusting through the whole process—I'm so glad I put my trust in you; to my editor, Rebecca Davis, who was able to see through the flaws to the very heart of what this book could be–I think you are full of a very special kind of magic. Thanks to the readers, for trusting me with your heart. Finally, and above all, thanks to God, for trusting me with this passion and inspiration and leading me here.